# YORK NOTES

*General Editors:* Professor A.N. Jeffares (*University of Stirling*) & Professor Suheil Bushrui (*American University of Beirut*)

Virginia Woolf

# MRS DALLOWAY

*Notes by John Mepham*
BA (OXON)

LONGMAN
YORK PRESS

D1392248

YORK PRESS
Immeuble Esseily, Place Riad Solh, Beirut.

LONGMAN GROUP UK LIMITED
*Longman House, Burnt Mill, Harlow,*
*Essex CM20 2JE, England*
*Associated companies, branches and representatives*
*throughout the world*

First published 1986
Third impression 1991

ISBN 0-582-02287-8

Produced by Longman Group (FE) Ltd.
Printed in People's Republic of China

# Contents

# Contents

# Part 1

# Introduction

## The author's life and works

Virginia Woolf was born in 1882. Her father, Sir Leslie Stephen, was a prominent Victorian intellectual who wrote books on history, biography and philosophy, but whose most lasting accomplishment was the huge sixty-three volume *Dictionary of National Biography* which he edited and to which he was the most prolific contributor for very many years. The large Stephen family lived in a house near Hyde Park in London. They were a comfortable, upper-middle-class family with social connections both with artists and writers (including the novelists Thackeray and Henry James) and with the social elite of judges, politicians and aristocracy.

As was normal at that time Virginia, as a girl, received no formal education. While her brothers were sent off to expensive schools and later to Cambridge University, she and her sister Vanessa had to make do with an informal education at home. Her sister, with whom she was exceptionally close all her life, became a well-known painter, one of a group through whom modern styles of painting were introduced into England. As for Virginia, her father encouraged her to read widely. She used his extensive library and decided when she was still a young girl that she wanted to follow her father and become a writer.

Virginia Stephen's life was deeply marked by a number of deaths in her family. Her much-loved mother died when Virginia was only thirteen years old. Her death destroyed for ever the secure, cheerful family life which Virginia had enjoyed until then. Her half-sister, Stella Duckworth, took over her mother's place in running the household but just two years later, when she had been married for only two months, she too suddenly died. Leslie Stephen died in 1904 after a long and painful illness through which he was nursed by Virginia. Two years later her brother Thoby, of whom she was very fond, suddenly died of typhoid fever which he caught while travelling in Greece. Virginia was still only twenty-four years old.

These deaths left Virginia Stephen badly shaken and deeply distressed. Her diaries show that she was obsessed with the memory of her dead parents for a very long time until, when she was in her mid-forties, she wrote a portrait of them and their marriage in her novel *To the Lighthouse*. After her mother's death Virginia's mental health deteriorated. She suffered her first serious breakdown in 1895 and her second after her father's death in 1904. At that time she was seriously incapacitated for many months. She suffered hallucinations and attempted to kill herself by throwing herself from a window. In 1910 and again in 1912 she was forced to spend some time in a private rest home. In 1913 she was again severely ill for many months and again attempted suicide. Her breakdowns became less severe after 1916, but for the rest of her life she was always liable to suffer from grave depression, nervous tension and physical illness. The madness of Septimus Warren Smith in *Mrs Dalloway* and his treatment at the hands of the doctors are closely based on Virginia Woolf's own experiences.

After their father's death the Stephen sisters set up home in Bloomsbury, a less fashionable district of London than the one in which they had previously lived. It is a district which, containing the University of London and the British Museum, is more associated with intellectual life and less with the luxurious living of the aristocracy. Their home became a meeting place for their brothers' friends from the University of Cambridge and there was formed what became known as the 'Bloomsbury Group'. This group of friends represented much of what was most modern both in their rejection of the oppressive taboos of Victorian moral and sexual life and in their cultural and intellectual interests and achievements. The Post-Impressionist paintings of the French artists Paul Cézanne (1839–1906) and Henri Matisse (1869–1954) were introduced to England by one of the group, the influential art critic and painter Roger Fry (1866–1934). Others read and translated into English the works of the Viennese founder of psychoanalysis, Sigmund Freud (1856–1939), and trained as psychoanalysts. In literature, the novelist E.M. Forster (1879–1970) and the poet T.S. Eliot (1888–1965) were associated with the group. Virginia Woolf was to become its most celebrated writer of fiction. A revolution in economic theory was to be accomplished by another member, John Maynard Keynes (1883–1946). The Bloomsbury Group was influential in English intellectual life for very many years.

In 1912 Virginia Stephen married Leonard Woolf (1880–1969), a young man who had been among her brother's friends at Cambridge. Unlike most of their circle he had to work for a living and he started a career in the colonial service as an administrator in Ceylon (now Sri Lanka). He gave up this career to marry Virginia Stephen and became an independent intellectual, a professional editor, writer and publisher (Leonard and Virginia Woolf founded the Hogarth Press in 1917 and it became an influential publishing house as well as a successful business). Leonard Woolf was active in the Labour Party and was involved in the campaign for the independence of India. Unlike many of the other members of the Stephen circle, he was a commonsensical, practical man who viewed the dominant culture with extreme scepticism and whose intellectual interests were more political than aesthetic. He recognised his wife's greatness as a writer and provided for her affectionate and admiring encouragement and support. They settled down to a reasonably comfortable life—Virginia having a private income. They had a home in London and later also a second home in the country. They employed servants. They ran their successful publishing business together. Their lives were a combination of hard work and the amusements of the wealthy. Virginia led a very active social life and cultivated relations with aristocratic women. Parties, like that given by Clarissa Dalloway, were very much part of her life. On medical advice, the Woolfs had no children.

Virginia Woolf is generally regarded as one of the finest English novelists. Her first novel, *The Voyage Out*, was published in 1915, but it was not until her third novel (*Jacob's Room*, published in 1922) that she began to write in her characteristically modernist narrative style, rejecting traditional forms of character and plot. *Mrs Dalloway* (1925) is in this line of development as are her famous later novels *To the Lighthouse* (1927), *The Waves* (1931) and *Between the Acts* (1941). She was a prolific writer. She published not only novels but also some very fine polemical feminist books (*A Room of One's Own*, 1929, and *Three Guineas*, 1938), books of literary essays (for example, *The Common Reader*, 1925, and *The Second Common Reader*, 1932). Many readers regard some of her writing that has only been published since her death as her finest, especially the autobiographical sketches in *Moments of Being* and her five-volume *Diary*.

Virginia Woolf died in 1941. Depressed and frightened by the thought that she was again on the verge of madness, she put rocks into the pockets of her coat and drowned herself in a river which ran near her home.

## Historical background

The period of Virginia Woolf's early life was one of profound social and cultural change. She was born into the Victorian world, and came to maturity as an author in the-modern world. In the Victorian world, certain central and unquestioned beliefs and values underpinned much of social and political life, beliefs and values which are summed up in words such as 'empire', 'civilisation', 'progress' and 'duty'. A particular way of understanding history accompanied these concepts and this way is mocked throughout *Mrs Dalloway*. For example, in the late Victorian world it could still seem totally natural that huge areas of the earth should be ruled from Britain. The British Empire was assumed to have a civilising and progressive mission. By the early 1920s, agitation for independence for India, the most glorious of imperial possessions, was well under way. In progressive circles, such as the Labour Party in which the Woolfs were active, the British Empire was now seen not as a natural phenomenon destined to last for ever, but as a transient historical phenomenon which was already showing signs of nearing the end of its life.

Part of the justification for imperial rule was the assumption of cultural superiority on the part of the British ruling class, and this was based on the belief that European political institutions and processes were rational and civilised. These beliefs were very severely shattered by the experience of the First World War of 1914–18. The Great War, as it was called, was seen by many as a demonstration not of advanced and superior European civilisation but of the most primitive and destructive forces of aggression and irrational hatred, as well as of gross political and military incompetence and official callousness and cruelty. Millions of soldiers died in the trenches for no rational cause. Freud, for example, in a correspondence with the greatest scientist of the modern age, Albert Einstein (1879–1955), on the causes of war— which was later published by the Woolfs at the Hogarth Press—argued that the war was the unleashing of pent-up instinctual aggression, that 'civilisation' was a thin veneer of deceptive behaviour covering over untamed brutalities. For those like Virginia Woolf and her pacifist friends, therefore, the war threw doubt on many of the central beliefs and values of ruling-class culture, and especially on military values and patriotism. The war did much to undermine the self-confidence and self-satisfaction of pre-war culture and to initiate a new age of European culture, the age of scepticism.

In fact, however, there was a long delay between the war and the assimilation of its lessons. Just as Septimus Warren Smith's madness is a delayed reaction to the horrors of the war, so there was in society generally resistance or incapacity to learn from the experience. This failure is a target for Virginia Woolf's mockery in *Mrs Dalloway*. There were too many who reacted to the war by gruffly exclaiming, as does Dr Holmes to Septimus, that there was nothing whatever the matter and that the best thing was to think about it as little as possible.

There were many other indications that a whole cultural world had irreversibly begun to change in this period. The Revolution that swept away a whole order in what in 1917 became the Soviet Union was an extreme form of this change, of the challenge to the old ruling classes of the world. In Britain, many of the institutions of the modern world had come into being and were about to take their place on the historical stage, including the mass trade unions and the Labour Party. Ramsay MacDonald became Britain's first Labour Prime Minister in January 1924, six months after the day of Mrs Dalloway's fictional party.

The other very notable series of changes that form an important part of the background to *Mrs Dalloway*, are those affecting the position of women in society, a topic of very great interest to Virginia Woolf. At the level of personal and social manners, the Bloomsbury Group prided themselves on having been part of that great cultural change which had swept away so much of the repressive prudery of Victorian society. As Peter Walsh remarks in *Mrs Dalloway*, so much more was possible for women in personal behaviour. What women could say, wear or do in public was not regulated by so many extreme conventional prohibitions as in earlier years. Peter Walsh notices, for example, the modern habit of wearing cosmetics, and young people being seen kissing in public. At the social level, many women had been drawn into work during the war and were to some extent able to gain entry into the universities and the professions (Miss Kilman is an example), though still in far fewer numbers than men. Opportunities were still far from equal for men and women, a state of affairs which is largely unchanged today.

At the level of politics, the Suffragettes, who campaigned for votes for women, had declared a truce in the battle for the vote in 1914 with the outbreak of the war, in order the better to contribute to the battle for their country. On 10 August 1914 all Suffragette prisoners were released, and their leader ordered a suspension of all militant activities. Patriotism first! In January 1918 six million women over the age of thirty at last won the right to vote in Britain. It was not until 1928 that full equality of voting rights between men and women was gained. Virginia Woolf worked for the Suffragettes in 1910, addressing envelopes.

Virginia Woolf's position in society was, then, a contradictory one. She came from a wealthy and privileged family background. She enjoyed the society of aristocratic women, though she also made fun of them. She had an inheritance, servants and two homes. On the other hand, she and her husband worked very hard, and regarded themselves as professional people. She thought of herself as an outsider in this male-dominated ruling stratum of society, since as a woman she had been excluded from education, and the power and privileges that go with it. She refused all honours that her fame brought her. All her life she loathed and feared male arrogance, pride and power. She denounced the tyranny of self-important men (Sir William Bradshaw in *Mrs Dalloway* being a famous example). In particular, she hated what she saw as male violence, whether it be the violence of imperial rule, of the State, of war, or the psychological violence of oppression within personal relationships.

This period also saw dramatic developments in art and literature. The English public were exposed to their first taste of modern painting in 1910 when Virginia's friend, the critic, Roger Fry, organised a Post-

Impressionist Exhibition in London (Leonard Woolf was employed as secretary to the Exhibition). She was fascinated by modernist painting and in particular by its ability to represent simultaneously in the picture things which were experienced from different perspectives and at different times. Painting was not restricted by the telling of a story, as novels seemed to be. She was excited by the idea of finding forms of writing that overcame these limitations, that opened up possibilities for fiction equivalent to those enjoyed in painting, for example the possibility of representing people or events from multiple points of view. She wanted to show how each moment in time does not simply pass by but lives on in the reverberations that it sets up in experience, memory and consciousness. Whereas the leaden circles of clock time rapidly fall away and dissolve into the air (as they repeatedly do in *Mrs Dalloway*), the moments of experience are like the waves and ripples that are set in motion when a pebble is thrown into a pool of water, which traverse great distances and affect all sorts of odd distant corners.

Virginia Woolf was enormously excited by the works of the French novelist Marcel Proust (1871–1922), whose novel *A la recherche du temps perdu* she read in 1922 as she was about to begin *Mrs Dalloway* (or *The Hours* as she then significantly called it). She shared with Proust a fascination with time and memory as subjects for exploration in writing, as well as his sense of social satire. Both his novel (conceived, of course, on a far greater scale than hers) and *Mrs Dalloway* climax at a party at which people from the past reappear and are made fun of. That year she also read *Ulysses* (1922) by the Irish novelist James Joyce (1882–1941) and had mixed feelings about it, though the idea of the novel as recording a single day in the lives of the characters and of the city may have been suggested by it. Other authors writing at the time who influenced her, especially in their development of the stream of consciousness narrative technique, were the English novelist Dorothy Richardson (1873–1957), whose novel *Pilgrimage* Virginia Woolf admired, though with some reservations, and the New Zealand writer of short stories, Katherine Mansfield (1888–1923), whom Virginia Woolf regarded as her main rival.

## The genesis of *Mrs Dalloway*

The characters Richard and Clarissa Dalloway first appear in Virginia Woolf's first novel *The Voyage Out* (1915). They are presented unsympathetically in that novel. Richard is a political reactionary who scoffs at the campaign for votes for women; Clarissa is a superficial snob wholly preoccupied with social rank and success. Virginia Woolf often enjoyed mixing in that world of hostesses and parties and was fascinated with its values and its power to attract people. In 1922 she decided to go back to Mrs Dalloway as a character, to develop her further, in order to explore that world. She set about writing a series of short stories, of which the first was called 'Mrs Dalloway in Bond Street', in which Clarissa goes shopping for gloves. She noted in her diary in October 1922 that she had formed the idea of writing a book to be called *The Party* or *At Home*, which was to consist of six or seven chapters converging on Mrs Dalloway's party at the end. Leonard Woolf remarked in his autobiography *Downhill All the Way* that 'the idea of a party always excited her, and in practice she was very sensitive to the actual mental and physical excitement of the party itself, the rise of temperature of mind and body, the ferment and fountain of noise'. The short stories were meant to examine what she called 'party consciousness', the ways that people at parties have of relating to each other and to themselves.

In the course of 1922 the project for a book of stories was abandoned and she set about writing a novel which seems to have been more ambitious in its intention, and more sombre in its mood. What she had in mind was a novel to be called *The Hours*. Some years later she revealed (in an introduction written in 1928 for the American edition of *Mrs Dalloway*) that 'Mrs Dalloway was originally to kill herself, or perhaps merely to die at the end of the party'. At some point late in 1922 she took the crucial step of introducing into the novel the theme of madness and began to work on the character of Septimus Warren Smith. By the middle of 1923 she was well into the writing of the novel that was to become *Mrs Dalloway*. By then the conception of the novel had become far more complex and much richer. She had added to the original interest in the hostess and the party a treatment of madness and an examination of society and its operation. She recorded in her diary on 19 June 1923: 'In this book I have almost too many ideas. I want to give life & death, sanity & insanity; I want to criticise the social system, & to show it at work, at its most intense.' The problem she now faced was that of integrating these disparate themes into one coherent novel via the character of Septimus Warren Smith. She incorporated into the novel rewritten versions of two of the stories that she had written for the earlier project, 'Mrs Dalloway in Bond Street' and 'The Prime Minister' (which is about the mystery person in the expensive car). The novel was finished in late 1924 and published in 1925.

After she had finished writing *Mrs Dalloway* Virginia Woolf returned to her project of a collection of stories around the theme of a party. She had already written several of these in 1922 and now, in the early months of 1925, she completed the sequence. It was finished by May that year but the stories were not published together as a book until long after Virginia Woolf's death. They are now available as *Mrs Dalloway's Party: A Short Story Sequence*. Her diaries, in which so much information about the writing of *Mrs Dalloway* and of all her other novels can be found, are now also all published. (For details see Part 5 below.)

## A note on the text

*Mrs Dalloway* was published on 14 May 1925 by the Hogarth Press, London. It has since been published in many languages and editions. Page references in these Notes refer to the paperback edition published by Triad Panther Books (Granada Publishing Ltd), London, in 1976 with numerous subsequent reprints.

# Part 2

# Summaries
*of* MRS DALLOWAY

## A general summary

The events narrated in *Mrs Dalloway* all take place on a single day in mid-June 1923. The novel opens with Clarissa Dalloway going out, at about ten o'clock in the morning, to buy flowers for a party she is to have at her house that evening. The novel closes as the party begins to fade at around midnight. Throughout the novel the reader is kept informed of the passing of time through the day, by the chiming of clocks, most often of Big Ben, the clock at the Houses of Parliament in Westminster, the district of London where the Dalloways live. Since the novel is not divided into chapters, this marking of the passage of time at intervals provides a regular and objective framework. The second objective framework within which everything takes place is that of London itself. The characters move around London. The city provides a space for interesting encounters and constantly changing perspectives. As the characters move around the city, all going about their private business, their paths cross or they witness the same events (such as the plane flying above them). The narration shifts from one character to another so that the events of the day are told from many points of view.

Contrasting with these predictable and objective frameworks of space and time are the subjective lives of each of the characters. Throughout the day, characters remember the past, fantasise about the future, speculate about each other and attend with greater or lesser degrees of success to the present. For much of the novel we follow the consciousness of Clarissa Dalloway. She prepares for her party, stops to mend a dress, and is then interrupted by the unexpected arrival of Peter Walsh, who loved her and wanted to marry her when she was young. Clarissa also attends to her seventeen-year-old daughter, Elizabeth, who goes out with her tutor, a woman whom Clarissa hates intensely. She sees her husband briefly in the afternoon. Later we find her at the beginning of her party, nervous in case it is a failure, and then again later as the evening goes by when she is more confident. Her party is interrupted when she happens to hear from Lady Bradshaw the news of the suicide of a young man called Septimus Warren Smith.

We have followed Septimus, a veteran of the war who is suffering from delayed shell-shock and is mentally unbalanced, and his Italian wife Lucrezia (or Rezia), in the course of their day. They have walked round London, sat in a park (where they happened to see Peter Walsh) waiting for a consultation with the distinguished doctor Sir William Bradshaw. Septimus is often delirious and his wife is deeply miserable, embarrassed when Septimus talks to himself in public, and terrified when he threatens to kill himself. Bradshaw immediately sees that he is severely ill and insists that he must go away to a nursing home. Later, at their home, the Warren Smiths find a few moments of happiness and normality but then their own doctor, Holmes, arrives and Septimus, refusing to submit to the power of the doctors, throws himself from his window and dies almost at once.

Weaving in and out of the account of the day as it is experienced by these characters, there is also recounted from time to time the consciousness of Peter Walsh, of Clarissa's husband Richard, a Conservative Member of Parliament, of Elizabeth and of her tutor, Miss Doris Kilman. Throughout the day characters remember a particularly significant time of their lives, a summer spent at Clarissa's family home, Bourton, when she was eighteen. The events of that summer had decisively influenced the entire course of her life, for she had then rejected Peter Walsh and decided to marry Richard Dalloway. She had also experienced a youthful infatuation with Sally Seton, a rebellious young girl who also reappears unexpectedly, turning up at Clarissa's party transformed into Lady Rosseter.

Clarissa Dalloway's attention during the day comes back again and again to thoughts about death. She has been ill and feels aware of age and of the rapid passing of her life. She thinks about the war and those who died in it. She thinks of her sister who died when she was young in a particularly horrible accident which Clarissa herself witnessed. She recites a quotation from Shakespeare: 'Fear no more the heat o' the sun/Nor the furious winter's rages', and this calms her and takes away the terror of death. (Septimus recites the same lines at a moment of repose during the afternoon.) When she hears of Septimus's death she strangely gains strength and reassurance from it.

At the close of the novel we find that we have not followed a story in the normal sense of the word. Very little has happened. We have circled around Mrs Dalloway so that she has been seen from many points of view, both internal and external, and now we have a sense that we are familiar with her, that we have come to know who she is. The novel ends with Clarissa simply appearing on the stairs at her party. 'For there she was.'

# Detailed summaries

The novel is not divided into chapters. Virginia Woolf divided it into sections by leaving an extra space between paragraphs at some points.

Unfortunately, these divisions are not the same in all editions of the novel. For convenience I have divided the book into the sections marked in the Triad Panther paperback edition, with the addition of a break between pages 51 and 52, and another after the end of the first paragraph on page 113. For those readers not using the Triad Panther edition, I have supplied the opening and closing words of each section so that the sections can be identified.

## Pages 5-14 (Mrs Dalloway said . . . were all *her* fault.)

Clarissa Dalloway goes out to buy flowers. She is preparing her house for a party. As she walks along she remembers Bourton, the family home of her youth, and the man who was then in love with her, Peter Walsh. He is expected to return from India soon. Big Ben strikes ten o'clock. It is June, the high season for upper-class sporting and social events. Mrs Dalloway meets an old friend, Hugh Whitbread, in St James's Park, and is again plunged into memories of her youth. She recalls her arguments with Peter Walsh and her decision not to marry him. Events and feelings from long ago still affect her intensely. She thinks of herself as having lost touch with the youthful vitality she once had, and thoughts about death begin to intrude, as they will do often during the day. In a bookshop window she reads a passage from Shakespeare: 'Fear no more the heat o' the sun/Nor the furious winter's rages.' This refrain will also be often repeated during the day. It has been a time of death for many people, of 'tears and sorrow', for the Great War is only recently over. As she walks up Bond Street, these themes are still on her mind and she thinks about illness, about her own body, about how she is finished with having children, and about an uncle who has recently died. She feels dissatisfied, empty: 'That is all', she says, thinking of her life, looking at a dead fish on a block of ice in a shop window.

Her thoughts shift to her daughter and to her daughter's dog, Grizzle, and her tutor, Miss Kilman. Mrs Dalloway hates Miss Kilman obsessively because she has introduced Elizabeth to religion. Her hatred is so strong that she is made quite unsteady by it. She arrives at the florists where Miss Pym and the flowers gradually calm her so that she recovers her composure. Suddenly there is a loud noise outside. It turns out to be a motor car.

NOTES AND GLOSSARY:
**veriest frumps:**   the most shabby and bad-tempered of women
**sandwich men:**   men carrying advertising boards
**Lords, Ascot, Ranelagh:** fashionable sporting and social locations in London (a cricket ground, a horse-racing track and a fashionable private club on the river, respectively)

**the Serpentine:**    a small lake in Hyde Park in London
**'Fear no more the heat o' the sun ... ':** a mourning song, sung over the body of Imogen in William Shakespeare's (1564-1616) play *Cymbeline*, Act IV, Scene 2
**distemper:**    a contagious disease of dogs
**mackintosh coat:**    a waterproof coat, named after its inventor

---

**Pages 14-27**    (The violent explosion ... writing a T, and O, an F.)

---

The expensive car outside the florist's shop is a mystery. Someone important is in it, but who? Among the crowd who speculate about the car are Septimus Warren Smith and his wife Lucrezia. Septimus is in a panic, thinking that the commotion in the street must be his fault. He talks aloud about killing himself. Mrs Dalloway comes out of the flower shop. She thinks it is the Queen in the car. The car moves away. As it moves through the streets the narrator, now heavily ironical in tone, recounts the crowd's patriotic reactions to it. As it passes, people think of the Empire, of the war and the Royal Family. As the car goes toward Buckingham Palace, London residence of the King, it passes many symbols of State and Empire – sentries, police, flags, statues of military heroes, a huge memorial to Queen Victoria. One of the crowd, a Mr Bowley, is overcome with emotion and weeps.

People stare at an aeroplane which is writing a message in the sky with smoke as it whirls overhead. It is eleven o'clock. The plane is advertising a brand of toffee. It is watched also by Septimus, now in Regent's Park. In his madness he takes the sky-writing to be a message to him, a revelation. Rezia is upset and confused because Holmes, their doctor, had said that there was nothing at all wrong with Septimus, and yet he carries on talking to himself and writing down delirious thoughts. He hears the birds singing in Greek, messages about death. He has an hallucination, believing that he sees in the Park a friend, Evans, who was killed in the war.

There is now a shift in point of view and we see the Warren Smiths as they are perceived by a passing young girl, Maisie Johnson. The narration shifts from one passer-by to another; each of them is watching the plane and idly musing on its significance.

NOTES AND GLOSSARY:
**Hurlingham:**    a private park where polo is played by rich people
**House of Windsor:** the British Royal Family
**shindy:**    slang word for an argument or quarrel
**White's:**    a private club
*Tatler*:    a magazine, founded in the early eighteenth century, documenting in news and fiction the lives of the upper classes

| | |
|---|---|
| **Bath chairs:** | wheelchairs for the old or infirm |
| **reft:** | an archaic word meaning 'deprived' |
| **decked out:** | adorned |

---

**Pages 27-44** ('What are they looking at?' . . . shut the door.)

Clarissa Dalloway arrives back home. She is disconcerted to find that her husband has been invited to lunch by Lady Bruton without her. She goes upstairs to her bedroom feeling herself to be old and sexless with little life left to her. She nowadays sleeps alone in an attic bedroom. She recognises that her marriage has not been passionate, that she tends to be cold and withdrawn, that she has sometimes failed her husband sexually.

Looking back, she can see that past moments of rapture, of warmth, have been with other women. She remembers Sally Seton whom she loved when she was a girl and with whom she experienced the most exquisite moment of her whole life. She panics, thinking how much she has aged. She has turned almost white since her recent illness. She takes a green dress downstairs and sits repairing it. She is soothed by the rhythm of her work and the repetitions of the phrases 'That is all' and 'Fear no more'.

Peter Walsh arrives unexpectedly, after five years away in India. They talk, excited and nervous with each other. Memories flood back. They are anxious about how their lives appear to each other. Peter Walsh announces that he is in love with a woman in India. Clarissa is scornful, irritated and jealous. They are interrupted when Elizabeth comes in. The clock strikes half past eleven.

NOTES AND GLOSSARY:

| | |
|---|---|
| **parasol:** | a small light umbrella used as a sun-shade |
| **linoleum:** | usually shortened to 'lino'; a floor covering |
| **the House:** | the House of Commons, one of the two Houses of the British Parliament |
| **William Morris:** | (1834-96) a socialist writer and designer |
| **'if it were now to die, 'twere now to be most happy':** | Othello's expression of his rapturous love for Desdemona in Shakespeare's *Othello*, Act II, Scene 1 |
| **mincing tones:** | an affectedly dainty or elegant manner of talking |
| **Hatfield:** | the family house of a well-known aristocratic family, the Cecils |
| **bandanna handkerchief:** | a large, colourful handkerchief, originally from India |

---

**Pages 44-51**   (Remember my party . . . and was muffled over.)

---

Peter Walsh goes off. Clarissa has disturbed and irritated him. That she refused to marry him all those years ago still hurts. The clock of St Margaret's church strikes half past eleven (after Big Ben has finished striking) and Peter has a clear but puzzling recollection of a moment of happiness with Clarissa. He feels tenderness and anxiety for her.

He walks up Whitehall. A parade of boys in military uniforms marches past, to perform a ceremony for those who were killed in the war. Peter Walsh muses on the renunciation of the flesh that is necessary for discipline and military glory. In his own life he has not been able to renounce the demands of the flesh. In light-hearted mood now, he follows a young woman through the streets, fantasising about her and enjoying the 'civilisation' that is life in London. He arrives in Regent's Park where he sits, smokes and dozes off to sleep.

NOTES AND GLOSSARY:

**Whitehall:**  the main location of government offices including the Ministry of Defence
**weedy:**  slang word meaning weak and feeble
**irreticences:**  a word made up by Virginia Woolf, the opposite of reticences, thus a disposition to speak freely
**Nelson, Gordon, Havelock:** British military heroes. Horatio, Lord Nelson (1758-1805), naval hero whose monument dominates Trafalgar Square commemorating his victory against the French; General George Gordon (1833-85), soldier and imperial administrator famous for his military campaigns in China and North Africa; Sir Henry Havelock (1795-1857), soldier, famous for his role in crushing the so-called 'Indian Mutiny'
**evanescent:**  rapidly disappearing
**air-balls:**  balls inflated with air for children to play with

---

**Pages 52-3**   (The grey nurse . . . solitary traveller make reply?)

---

Peter Walsh's dream; a series of puzzling images. A solitary traveller in a forest has visions of a giant figure in the trees, of a mother who has lost her sons in war and of a woman clearing a breakfast table.

---

**Pages 53-9**   (So the elderly nurse . . . He never saw her again.)

---

Peter Walsh wakes suddenly saying 'The death of the soul'. He remembers that he has sometimes felt that Clarissa is cut off from life, that she is timid, prudish, cold. He recalls the moment at Bourton when he realised that she would marry Richard Dalloway. He knows now that he did make absurd demands on her, that he was always making scenes and starting quarrels. He suffered terribly. He recalls their final talk vividly: it has mattered more than anything in his life. She was unyielding. It was over.

NOTES AND GLOSSARY:
**ticketing:** labelling
**fiddle-strings:** violin strings

---

**Pages 59-84** (It was awful . . . looking not quite so kind.)

---

Peter Walsh remembers that awful experience of rejection. But he turns his attention back to Regent's Park where Lucrezia Warren Smith is walking and suffering, full of resentment and self-pity at having to tolerate her husband's embarrassing behaviour. Septimus is sitting on a bench raving. He has grandiose visions of himself as a saviour possessed of a secret message to mankind. He hallucinates. He has moments of visionary joy. He mistakes Peter Walsh for his dead friend Evans.

A clock strikes eleven forty-five. Walsh walks past and takes the Warren Smiths to be a young couple having an argument. He is thinking how much things have changed since the war. Behaviour, particularly between the sexes, is more relaxed now. He remembers Sally Seton and her arguments long ago with the snobbish and old-fashioned Hugh Whitbread. His train of thought again turns to Clarissa. Though he denies to himself that he is still in love with her, his thoughts circle round her obsessively, trying to sum her up—her marriage, her views about death, her sense of fun, her daughter—he regards her from every angle. As he leaves the park he hears an ancient beggar-woman singing a song celebrating her love for a man long dead. He gives her a coin. The Warren Smiths also pass by, on their way to an appointment with a doctor.

There follows (pages 75-84) a long section which is unusual in this novel in that it is not narrated from the point of view of one of the characters. An impersonal narrator tells the story of Septimus's life. He came to London as a young man, fell in love and worked as an estate agent's clerk. He joined the army at the outbreak of war and survived physically unscathed, unlike his friend Evans who was killed just before the war ended. In Milan after the war he married Lucrezia, an innkeeper's daughter. He began to suffer attacks of panic. He had no feelings and experienced everything as though behind a pane of glass. Back in England he returned to work, but his life had changed. He rejected sex (whereas Rezia badly wanted to have children). One day he gave in to his despair and terror and asked for help, but Dr Holmes could find nothing wrong with him. Septimus became suicidal. He began to hallucinate. Holmes being useless, Septimus and his wife had arranged to consult Sir William Bradshaw of Harley Street.

NOTES AND GLOSSARY:
**habit of paint:**     the habit of using cosmetics
**those poor girls in Piccadilly:** prostitutes
**picked up for an old song:** bought very cheaply
**The steam coal was a little too strong for her:** she found it hard to tolerate her husband's background in a family of coal
merchants
**fogies:**     very old-fashioned people
**Huxley and Tyndall:** Thomas Henry Huxley (1825-95), a distinguished
Victorian scientist who also wrote popular works
on religious, moral and social subjects; best known
as a champion of Charles Darwin's (1809-82)
theory of evolution. John Tyndall (1820-93), distinguished Victorian geologist and physicist who
also wrote a famous address on religious belief
**Elizabeth was 'out':** Elizabeth had been introduced into 'society' after
presentation at Court
**coppers:**     coins of low denomination
**in a funk:**     incapacitated by fear
**Harley Street:**     location of expensive, specialist physicians' con-
sulting rooms

---

**Pages 84-113**    (It was precisely twelve o'clock . . . want to cry.)

---

It is midday. The Warren Smiths are with Sir William Bradshaw, a wealthy, powerful doctor of high reputation. He interviews Septimus and, unlike Holmes, he immediately understands that he is severely ill. Septimus is on the verge of explaining how he feels but neither the doctor nor his wife listen to him. Bradshaw announces that Septimus will be compelled to go to a 'home', an asylum. He explains to Rezia that the law permits him to insist on Septimus's being taken away because he has threatened to kill himself. He refuses to use the word 'madness', but says that Septimus has lost his sense of proportion. He tries to create confidence and trust in his patient; but the irony makes it clear that he has no sympathy or real understanding at all. The Warren Smiths leave.

There follows (pages 88-91) an extraordinary section, a fierce, mock-ing attack on Bradshaw, an angry denunciation of him. It is not one of the characters who speaks. Behind the narrator's voice one can detect

Virginia Woolf's own anger at her treatment at the hands of doctors. But the attack is against all forms of tyranny and domination. For, it says, Bradshaw has simply made himself rich by exercising power over people for his own benefit. Bradshaw is really governed by the Goddess Conversion, which is to say by the desire to subordinate others to his will. He forces everyone to obey him. He claims to be motivated by humanitarian concern, by values such as love and self-sacrifice, but in fact he is driven by the desire to dominate, to subdue all opposition. His wife submitted to him years ago and is now completely subservient. He attempts to make his patients accept his authority but if that fails he locks them up. He is a tyrant.

Septimus and Rezia walk away. It is one thirty. Nearby, in Oxford Street, the complacent Hugh Whitbread is looking at socks in a shop window. His achievements in life have been very modest, and yet he is described (with strong irony) as magisterial, as magnificent, as he looks at the socks. He meets Richard Dalloway, and they go in to Lady Bruton's house for lunch. Lady Bruton is also treated ironically. Fun is made of the ceremonial meals of the rich, at which food appears as if by magic, the money spent on it and the labour of cooking it all being kept invisible. The superiority of the wealthy hostess is just a conjuring trick. Fun is also made of Lady Bruton's inherited military manner, of her rather masculine involvement in politics and her strong patriotism.

The three of them chat about Peter Walsh and Richard decides that after lunch he will go to Clarissa and tell her that he loves her. A pompous letter to *The Times* newspaper on the subject of a scheme to encourage emigration is written by Whitbread for Lady Bruton. He is able to put things in order whereas she cannot think clearly at all. When it is done, the men leave and Lady Bruton goes up to her room to snore majestically on her sofa.

The men visit a jeweller's shop. Richard is suffering from after-lunch lethargy, and is slow and indecisive. While the pompous Hugh Whitbread argues with the jeweller's assistant, Dalloway becomes impatient and remembers his project of going back home to see his wife. The talk of Peter Walsh has roused in him some feeling (about which he and his wife never talk) of gratitude and amazement at the miracle of Clarissa being his wife. He sets off to buy flowers for her and again resolves to tell her that he loves her.

At three o'clock he walks into his house and presents Clarissa with a bunch of roses. He finds it impossible to say that he loves her but she understands what he is thinking. He spends a short, happy time with her before setting off for the House of Commons to work. Clarissa is ignorant about and uninterested in politics. She is resting and is preoccupied with preparations for her party. She wonders why it is that she likes to give parties, to bring people together, even though both

Richard and Peter criticise her for it. She decides that it is because she likes life, and that giving parties is an offering, though an offering to whom she does not know. Her mind drifts among the various themes of her day and eventually back to the question of death. She is interrupted by Elizabeth.

At this point we have, for the first time, narration from the point of view of Doris Kilman. She is an educated but bitter and self-pitying woman of lower-class origins. She lost her teaching job unfairly during the war. She suffers from violent, turbulent emotions which threaten to overwhelm her. She has experienced a religious conversion. Like Sir William Bradshaw, she wants to dominate people. She has a powerful desire to overcome Mrs Dalloway, to expose her as a trivial fool. But unlike the doctor, she has neither the wealth nor the social position and power to achieve this mastery, and her religion is used in an attempt to calm her frustration. She loves Elizabeth Dalloway. Miss Kilman and Mrs Dalloway, hating each other, confront each other on the stairs until Mrs Dalloway, finding her common and ridiculous, laughs at her and humiliates her.

Clarissa, worked up emotionally by seeing her daughter going off with the hated Miss Kilman, reflects that love and religion are both cruel and detestable; they both lead to the desire to tyrannise and dominate, to convert. As she stands by her window, she can see an old lady in the house opposite who climbs her stairs and moves about from one room to another. She is alone. For Clarissa, she is a figure of independence and privacy, things of high value which love and religion threaten to destroy.

NOTES AND GLOSSARY:

**Eton:** the most famous private boys' school in England, at which the sons of the elite are educated

**shindy:** a brawl

**At Hyde Park Corner on a tub:** at Speakers' Corner, Hyde Park, traditionally a place for public speaking by those with strong views who wish to gain converts

**dragoons:** cavalry soldiers

**Lovelace, Herrick:** Richard Lovelace (1618–58) and Robert Herrick (1591–1674), both lyric poets

**had ... come a cropper:** had failed miserably

**shallop:** a small fishing boat

**were whelmed:** a dialect word: became covered over with water

**costermongers:** people who sell goods from a stall in the street

**offering:** a ceremonial gift, usually in a religious context

**the Friends:** a religious sect, the Society of Friends or Quakers, founded in the mid-seventeenth century

**extension lecturing:** giving lectures organised by the university for the general public rather than for university students

---

**Pages 113-34**  (Love destroyed too . . . So that was Dr Holmes.)

---

Clarissa continues to think about love. She finds it degrading and destructive. It leads sensitive people (Peter Walsh is an example) to do foolish things. As the clock strikes half past three, Clarissa thinks also about religion. People think that religion solves mysteries but it does not solve the main mystery which is the separation, the distance between each individual, which neither love nor religion can overcome. She is still watching the old woman in the house opposite, moving about from one room to another.

We shift (page 114) to the point of view of Miss Kilman in the street. She is still suffering from the humiliation of being laughed at and she collapses emotionally into a state of defeat and self-loathing. She hates her own body, her ugliness. She cannot believe that she will ever be loved. She tries to control herself by thinking of the religious lessons of her friend the preacher, the Reverend Edward Whittaker. She and Elizabeth go into a big department store (the Army and Navy Stores) to buy clothes and have tea. Eating is one of Miss Kilman's few pleasures.

The narrator (page 116) adopts Elizabeth's point of view for the first time. She is fascinated by her clever, university-educated history teacher but she cannot help finding her disgusting and overpowering. Miss Kilman has introduced Elizabeth to history, to social problems, to the idea of professions for women, but when she eats or grasps flowers she seems graceless and threatening. She is an example of everything that Clarissa fears about love, for she wishes to clasp Elizabeth to herself, to possess and absorb her with the same unappealing, greedy appetite that she has for the cream cakes. The description of Miss Kilman at tea focuses on her clutching hands, thick fingers and threatening mouth. As Elizabeth prepares to leave, Miss Kilman, in a tactless and embarrassing effort to stop her going, pours out her unhappiness and hatred and self-loathing in a desperate and repulsive attempt to win Elizabeth's sympathy. She wants Elizabeth's affection. She attempts to force it out of her. Elizabeth, like a simple, nervous young animal confronted with a monster, rushes away.

Miss Kilman, like a great wounded beast, blunders out of the store and, completely absorbed in her misery, goes to Westminster Abbey to pray. In the quiet of the church she fights against her impulses and obsessions.

Elizabeth has gone off by herself. She is a self-conscious seventeen-year-old adolescent, uncomfortable under people's admiring gaze. She would be happier, she thinks, alone with her father and dogs, in the country. She resists growing up. She sets off on a bus and entertains herself with a child's fantasy of being on a pirate ship. But then she begins to think about her future—what is she to become? As she passes the big, stately government offices at Somerset House, she finds herself attracted to the idea of having a career, of being a modern working woman, unlike her mother, of having a profession. She is passing through the heart of London, surrounded by banks, government offices, newspaper buildings, and she becomes excited by a vision of the great procession of life which carries everyone along in its stream, and by the idea of the generations of Dalloway women who worked in public service. Ironically, the noisy procession with military music, which has inspired her fantasies, is a demonstration of the unemployed. She gets on a bus to go home. She is still in a dreamy mood and she indulges in sentimental, adolescent fantasies about great palaces in the clouds.

The narration shifts (page 124) to Septimus Warren Smith who is sitting on a sofa in his sitting-room, which happens to overlook the same scene that Elizabeth is enjoying outside. He is calm, content. His thoughts strangely echo those of Mrs Dalloway earlier in the day (pages 36-7) when she was sitting relaxed on her sofa mending her dress. 'Fear no more', he thinks, with a vision of a summer's day with waves breaking and dogs barking. He has lost his fear. Shakespeare's poetry (dismissed scornfully by Dr Holmes as it had been earlier by Richard Dalloway) soothes him. Rezia sits at a table making a hat and they begin to chat quite normally. They joke and laugh together, designing the hat, reading a newspaper. Septimus takes an interest in ordinary, everyday things such as cricket scores. Rezia feels comfortable with him as she used to when they first met. She feels that she can say anything that comes into her head. They remember Bradshaw. Septimus wants to get out all his accumulated writings and drawings and to burn them all. Everything seems so normal. Rezia promises that nothing will separate them. But at this moment Dr Holmes appears. Rezia tries to keep him out but he forces his way into the room. Septimus opens the window and throws himself out, down onto the railings below. He dies almost at once. As the clocks strike six o'clock, Rezia goes into a disturbed drugged sleep.

NOTES AND GLOSSARY:

**troublously:** an archaic word: agitated

**oil and colour shop:** a shop that sell paints and other materials for artists

**K.C.:** King's Counsel; a high judiciary office (held by barristers appointed as counsel to the Crown on the nomination of the Lord Chancellor)

**Pages 134-46**   (One of the triumphs . . . his pocket-knife.)

As Peter Walsh walks back to his hotel, the ambulance carrying away Septimus's body passes by. For Walsh it represents 'civilisation', the ability and organisation to get things done quickly and efficiently, at which he has marvelled at various points during the day. He thinks about life and death and experiences a moment of some emotional intensity. He is susceptible to such moments of heightened emotion and they have shaped his life.

As so often during this day, Peter Walsh now finds himself recalling the excitements of his relationship with Clarissa Dalloway when they were young. He remembers her theories about death–how perhaps intense moments indicate that there is something deeper in a person than the everyday self, something which might survive after death. Certainly, he decides, it is a mystery how his whole life has been influenced by Clarissa even though their actual meetings have always been painful and uncomfortable. He reaches his hotel and finds that Clarissa has sent him a letter.

There follows (pages 138-9) a short sketch of Peter Walsh and what it is about him that makes him attractive to women, for example to Daisy whom he is planning to marry. She is only twenty-four and, Peter thinks, is so much more straightforward than Clarissa, and willing, unlike the frigid Clarissa, to give him everything. Peter is very unsure what to do about Daisy. As he settles down in his impersonal hotel room, he finds himself thinking that perhaps he should not marry her. Perhaps it would be best for him to retire and write some modest little book (as he has planned to since his youth). Would it not be best for Daisy if she forgot him?

He goes down to dinner and gains some contentment at being approved of by a party of respectable strangers who strike up a conversation with him. He decides that he will after all go to Clarissa's party, to enjoy the company and the gossip. He sits outside the hotel smoking and watches the city change as people prepare for the evening or pass on their way to eat or to the cinema. He is reminded yet again of how much things have changed, how differently people can behave now, how oppressive it all was when he was young, especially for the women. He buys and reads a newspaper, reading about the day's trivial news, the weather and the cricket scores. As happens throughout the novel, Peter shifts his attention effortlessly from the superficial events of the day to his deepest memories and strongest feelings, from surface impressions or fantasies to complex moods or inner discussions and uncertainties.

Peter Walsh sets off to walk to the Dalloways, pleased with the atmosphere of excitement in the city, as young people go about enjoying themselves. He notes another modern phenomenon, young couples kissing in the shade of the trees. He observes and enjoys the city, until he arrives at the Dalloways' house.

NOTES AND GLOSSARY:

**draggling:** walking around slowly and listlessly

**the Halls:** the music halls, places of popular entertainment

**the Bodleian:** the library of the University of Oxford

**come up to the scratch:** do what is expected or demanded

**the great revolution of Mr Willett's summer time:** William Willett (1856-1915) campaigned for the introduction of British Summer Time, when clocks are advanced by one hour during the summer months; it was introduced after his death, in 1916

---

**Pages 146-65**   (Lucy came running... came in from the little room.)

---

This section starts with the army of servants in the Dalloway household, as guests finish dinner and begin to arrive for the party. Virginia Woolf, unlike her character Lady Bruton, is not going to hide away the money and the servants' labour which make all the entertainment possible. We catch glimpses of three maids, a cook, two women on the door and at the cloakroom, and Mr Wilkins who announces the guests as they arrive. Peter Walsh comes in and witnesses this ceremonial greeting of the guests. He sees Clarissa at her worst, playing at being a grand lady, effusive and insincere.

In fact she is nervous, worrying that the party will be a failure and feeling defensive under Peter Walsh's critical eye. Gradually the party warms up until at a certain moment Clarissa sees that she can relax, recognising that the party has now started properly and is going to be all right. She is receiving the guests as they arrive, when a Lady Rosseter, of whom Clarissa has not heard, is announced. She turns out to be Sally Seton, the unconventional and rebellious girl whom Clarissa loved at Bourton, and whom Clarissa, Richard and Peter have each recalled during the day. She is married to a wealthy man, lives in Manchester and has five sons, which is all to say that she is now completely unlike her youthful self, for she is now conventional, unglamorous and rather ordinary.

The Prime Minister arrives. He is described with heavy irony, for he is a very unimpressive, ordinary-looking person (he is said to look like a grocer) who by virtue of his position signifies the majesty of the State and the dignity of English history and Empire. The snobbish Lady Bruton and Hugh Whitbread gather round him and the detached and sceptical Peter Walsh looks on with amused contempt. He can see that Clarissa is now at ease, in her element, and has lost her coldness and reserve.

In fact, however, Clarissa is thinking about the superficiality and hollowness of her social triumph. She recognises that it does not engage the emotions deeply, does not have the satisfaction, for example, of her hatred of Miss Kilman. As if in perfect illustration of this, there follows a series of comic portraits of the minor guests, each of dubious merit. There is Sir Harry, a mediocre, academic painter; the arrogant Professor Brierly, an expert on Milton; and Lord Gayton, an aristocratic sportsman and representative of the energetic but mindless young people of the upper classes, who are all vivacious but inarticulate, who as Clarissa observes can play cricket and dance but have no use for the resources of the English language. They are glamorous but dull.

Fun is now made of some of the imperial old ladies. There is Clarissa's old Aunt Helena Parry who, a very long time ago, wrote a book on the orchids of Burma, and who is treated with gentle mockery. There is the formidable Lady Bruton, of military bearing and unthinking patriotism, who is seen with a more critical eye. Clarissa moves among them all, noticing Peter Walsh and Sally Seton chatting together when Sir William Bradshaw and his wife arrive.

Clarissa fears and dislikes Bradshaw. He has seemed to her to be a man without sympathy or understanding. He discusses with Richard Dalloway the problem of the deferred effects of shell-shock (which is the label given by the doctors to the condition from which Septimus Warren Smith had suffered), which is to be debated in Parliament. Bradshaw tells Richard of Septimus's case. Lady Bradshaw meanwhile tells the story of Septimus's suicide to Clarissa. All day death has been forcing its way into her thoughts, and now here it is at her party. She retreats to a room where she can be by herself.

Clarissa thinks about Septimus's suicide. She compares it in her mind with the occasion when she had thrown a coin into the Serpentine. This was the most that she had ever achieved by way of a spontaneous gesture of extravagance or defiance. She senses that Septimus, by throwing away his life, may have preserved something valuable, something that lies hidden beneath all the chatter, insincerity and corruption. Perhaps his death was an attempt to communicate his refusal to give up something that he believed in. Had he, in dying, preserved some great rapture? (Clarissa remembers her own rapture, of long ago.) His death was also a resistance, a refusal to allow himself to be forced, dominated by the obscure evil of Sir William Bradshaw, a refusal to accept the intolerable life that the doctors wanted to impose on him. Clarissa knows that the suicidal young man was not so very different from the rest of us, from herself, for example, for she also suffers from a great fear which could destroy her.

Clarissa again watches the old woman in the house opposite, the independent survivor, just living quietly by herself. Three elements that have recurred often during the day are now brought together in a powerful combination—the old woman goes about her life alone, the clock strikes to remind Clarissa of the passage of time, and she chants to herself, 'Fear no more the heat of the sun'. All day there have been hints at some solemnity, some revelation hidden behind all the noise and chatter of the day, and in this brief moment we sense the presence to Clarissa of some deeper experience of time and self, some ceremony of grief for the loss of the past, perhaps some victory for Septimus and Clarissa against the forces of ignorance and prejudice. But it is a very brief moment, for consciousness will always keep moving and rediscover its attachments to the things of the everyday world; as the sound of the clock's striking ceases, Clarissa recalls herself to her duties as hostess. She must go back to her party.

NOTES AND GLOSSARY:
**Bill:** proposal for a new law placed before Parliament
**Commons:** House of Commons
**missed his eleven:** failed to get into the cricket team

---

**Pages 165-72** ('But where is Clarissa?' . . . For there she was.)

---

In this final section, Clarissa and her party are observed by Peter Walsh and Sally Seton who sit talking together and waiting for Clarissa to come to them. Through Sally Seton, now Lady Rosseter, we get yet another, different perspective on Clarissa and on those episodes of so many years ago when they had all meant so much to each other. As throughout the day, we keep coming back to the same past events and the same people and seeing them from fresh points of view. We hear Sally's views about Clarissa's character and life; she has never understood or sympathised with Clarissa's choice of Richard Dalloway. Peter Walsh gives to Sally a version of his own life story. Each time a story is told the emphases are different, the meanings not quite the same. His relations with Clarissa, Peter now says, have spoiled his life.

There is no fixed and final story that the characters tell to themselves about their lives. Over and above all the talk and all the attempts to define each other's characters and the shape of their lives, there is something else, something the force of which Peter feels as Clarissa appears, something that goes beyond all the words and which causes him still to feel terror, ecstasy and extraordinary excitement, after all these years and all the disappointments. 'For there she was.'

NOTES AND GLOSSARY:

| | |
|---|---|
| **Emily Brontë:** | (1818-48) novelist and poet; author of *Wuthering Heights* |
| **Windsor:** | Windsor Castle, one of the residences of the Royal Family |
| **a perfect goose:** | a silly or foolish person |

# Part 3

# Commentary

## Narrative style

### Story

*Mrs Dalloway* does not tell an exciting story; very little happens to the characters. The reader does not suffer an urgent desire to know what happens next. In most traditional novels the emphasis is on some interesting story. In some books it is the story of a process, such as growing up. In others, it is the story of a discovery, for example the unravelling of a mystery (who committed the crime?). Some novels tell the story of the gaining of success, culminating in a marriage or a victory. *Mrs Dalloway* is none of these. For example, the novel does tell us about long-standing problems (should Clarissa have married Peter Walsh? Does Peter Walsh have a flawed character?). But at the end of the novel, these problems are just as unresolved as they were at the beginning. It could be said that the other main story in the novel, that of Septimus Warren Smith's struggle with his madness and with his doctors, does have a culmination; it ends in Septimus's death and defeat. But even this apparently definitive ending, the ending of his life, does not have the quality that story endings so often traditionally have, of having a clear message attached, some lesson that we are expected to learn. Septimus's death raises more questions than it answers—are we to see it as a victory for the brutal doctors and their insensitivity, or are we to see it, as Clarissa does, as a successful defiance of their arbitrary and ignorant power, and as a successful communication or assertion of value?

The interest in *Mrs Dalloway*, then, is not so much in the stories, the destinies, of the various characters, as in their subjective lives, the mental processes with which they each react to events. As they move about London, meeting each other and performing their tasks, they are all living very shifting, complex, subjective lives with streams of memories, fantasies, fears, excitements and forebodings, fluctuating moods and changeable feelings. The emphasis in the novel is on these movements of consciousness, or streams of consciousness as they have been called.

## Multiple points of view

In the course of the novel we do get to know quite a lot about the main characters, about their lives and about how they usually think and behave. But, again in contrast with many more traditional novels, we do not finish up with a definite judgement on the characters or a finalised sense of who they are. Many questions about them remain unanswered at the end of the book and many areas of ambiguity remain unresolved. For example, Peter Walsh at one point talks about the death of Clarissa's soul as his way of summing up some essential lack in her. But is he right? Other characters talk about Peter Walsh's unconventionality as a weakness, but he himself thinks about it as a strength. Who is right? What produces this uncertainty?

Often in traditional novels, our feeling of having arrived at a definite judgement, at a certainty as to someone's character, derives from the fact that the characters are described from what appears to be an authoritative point of view. The narrator of a traditional novel often seems to be in a position to tell us just who everyone is and what their actions all mean. For some reason we trust what the narrator says. We are usually content to go along with the convention of this so-called omniscient narrator, who not only tells the reader what happens but also tells us the significance of everything that happens and of everything the characters say or do. In contrast, in *Mrs Dalloway* each of the main characters is described and interpreted from many points of view, as they are seen and remembered by each other. So our sense of them is very shifting and unstable. There does not seem to be any single, privileged, objective and external point of view from which the whole truth about, say, Clarissa Dalloway, can be told. Rather, there are many points of view, many different reactions to her, and we, like a jury, listen to them all and then try to make up our minds. We hear what Peter Walsh used to think about Clarissa when they were young and he was in love with her. We hear also how he reacts to her now, at various points during the day. To this are added the reactions and interpretations of Sally Seton, Richard Dalloway and Miss Kilman. We even get short glimpses of her from the point of view of very minor characters who appear only briefly, like Lucy the maid or Scrope Purvis (page 5). Moreover, we are also given her own view of herself; the narrative sometimes adopts her point of view and tells us how she subjectively experiences herself, how she views her own life and, of course, how she views the other characters.

Mrs Dalloway notices how she assembles herself into one single, definite person in order to appear in public; she uses her mirror in an effort to draw all the different parts together to make a coherent image of herself (page 34). But she knows that, in reality, this singleness, this definiteness and coherence, are an illusion which is created by hiding away all the unacceptable sides of herself, her 'faults, jealousies, vanities, suspicions'. The novel tries to assemble her not as a single, coherent character, but as a complicated, contradictory person, many-faceted, and observed from many points of view. The picture that we finally have of her, and of the other characters, is consequently a rich and complex one just because it leaves all sorts of questions about them unsettled. The series of views of Mrs Dalloway does not pretend to be complete, but only to have created a strong sense of her presence or of familiarity. The end of the novel is not a final judgement, 'That is who she is', but a sense of her presence, 'For there she was'.

Of course, not all of the characters are treated with this patience and tolerance, this sense of leaving things about them unresolved. There are two particular characters about whom Virginia Woolf seems to have been unable to reserve judgement, so strong were her negative feelings. With these two characters we find that she reverts to traditional, objective, omniscient narration. They are Miss Kilman and Sir William Bradshaw. The narrator tells us in no uncertain terms what to think about each of them.

## The past

The past life and experiences of each of the characters, of course, still affect his or her present life. But in this novel the past lives of the characters are not narrated in chronological order; rather they emerge gradually, in fragments, as memories. At the very beginning of the book we immediately learn something about Mrs Dalloway's past life. As soon as she sets off shopping she has flashes of memory of the early morning air at Bourton when she was young and she half remembers something that Peter Walsh had said. Virginia Woolf's image for this way of narrating the past is that it is as if behind the present moment each of the characters has a series of caves. These caves, which are the past experiences or episodes in their lives, are connected to each other by tunnels, and these tunnels come to the surface as memories. Since the characters have shared episodes in their lives, their tunnels or memories interconnect. Virginia Woolf wrote in her diary (30 August 1923) about what she called her 'discovery' of how to construct the past lives of her characters: 'I dig out beautiful caves behind my characters: I think that gives exactly what I want; humanity, humour, depth. The idea is that the caves shall connect and each comes to daylight at the present moment.'

A partial exception to this method of narrating the past is to be found in the case of Septimus Warren Smith. We find (pages 75-84) that Septimus's past life is narrated here by the more traditional method; it is told like a story by an omniscient narrator rather than being given as a series of disconnected, fragmentary flashbacks. Earlier in the book (pages 22-4, for instance) the reader has already been introduced to some episodes of Septimus's past by Virginia Woolf's method of 'tunnelling'. A good exercise is to compare and contrast how we gradually come to know about the crucial episodes that have helped to shape all of her subsequent life, in the case of Clarissa Dalloway, with how we come to learn about the crucial episodes in Septimus's case.

One consequence of presenting the past as a network of interconnecting caves is that the emphasis can quite naturally be felt to fall on those past episodes that are most repeated or most dwelt on in the present with strong feeling. But it is important to realise that the past does not only provide us with information about the route by which characters have arrived at the present. It is too easy to think of all past moments as being connected together in a single line, each one pregnant with all those that are to follow. Past moments are pregnant not only with the future which actually came about, but also with possible futures which failed to come into being. Past moments point towards routes which we might have taken but, for some reason, did not take. In Clarissa's case, the route to the present was through her choice of Richard Dalloway as her husband. But there are other experiences which remind her of other possible paths that her life might have taken, that were real, potential futures for her, but which she rejected (marriage with Peter Walsh). She is also reminded of kinds of experience which she once valued highly (which in fact she still values highly in memory, nostalgically) but which have had little place in her subsequent life (her passionate attachment to Sally Seton). So the past is not just a series of events on a route leading to the present, but a series of crossroads at which one path was taken and others rejected, some possibilities kept alive and others eliminated.

## Free indirect speech

Another major narrative technique used a great deal in *Mrs Dalloway* is a particular method of representing what the characters are saying and thinking, which is called 'free indirect speech'. In direct speech, a narrator directly quotes the words of a character, and this is usually signalled by the use of quotation marks. For example: '"I have five sons!" she told him.' An alternative method of narration is called indirect speech. In this method the narrator tells us about what a character has said or thought without necessarily reproducing the exact words used. In this case, for example, the speech could be reported thus: 'She told him that she had five boys.' Both the tense and the pronoun are different from what they were in direct speech ('she had' instead of 'I have').

These two narrative styles, direct and indirect speech, are the styles most commonly used in nineteenth-century novels for representing the speech and thought of fictional characters. In Virginia Woolf's work (and in that of some other modern writers such as Henry James and Katherine Mansfield) a third narrative style becomes of central importance. This is free indirect speech, in which the narrator sticks closely enough to the character's own words to give both the gist of what was said or thought and also the verbal style of it without necessarily claiming to reproduce it word for word. This method is used repeatedly throughout *Mrs Dalloway*. Its characteristic quality is that the tense and pronoun are typical of indirect speech but the sense of being given a quotation is more like direct speech, so this style has some of the character of each of the others. For example (page 82):

'So you're in a funk,' he said agreeably, sitting down by his patient's side. He had actually talked of killing himself to his wife, quite a girl, a foreigner, wasn't she? Didn't that give her a very odd idea of English husbands? . . . For he had had forty years' experience behind him; and Septimus could take Dr Holmes's word for it—there was nothing whatever the matter with him.

The first phrase is directly quoted, but thereafter Dr Holmes's speech is given in free indirect speech. This allows the narrator to capture Holmes's style of speaking and thinking and hence to make fun of it. For example, in this passage his smug self-confidence, very limited intelligence and absurd patriotism are all mimicked and made fun of. This has all been achieved very efficiently, because the narrator has not had to give a full reproduction of the conversation; we have an edited version which highlights the important points in the character's speech and retains his verbal idiom.

A second aspect of free indirect speech is that it allows the narrator to articulate, to put into words and images, aspects of the character's experience and consciousness which for the character remain non-verbal or which are not fully spelled out in words. Look, for example, at the passage where Mrs Dalloway goes up to her bedroom feeling old and sexless, like a nun (page 29). The narration keeps very close to the stream of Clarissa's thoughts, but we are not to imagine that she actually speaks to herself inwardly in exactly the words that are given. It is as if the narration were spelling out her thoughts, ideas and images, which for her quite likely remained fragmented and non-verbal. For example, the very clear and powerful images of the narrow bed and the virginity which clung to her like a sheet are not necessarily to be read as

Clarissa's own verbalised images, but as images which do poetically express what she thought. This suggests that we have to take the metaphor of the stream of consciousness rather carefully: since the narrator both edits and provides an elaboration in metaphors of the character's consciousness, it would be a mistake to read the words on the page as a word-for-word transcription of the character's own interior monologue. In this respect, Virginia Woolf's narrative technique gives quite different results from, for example, those of James Joyce in *Ulysses*. She writes nothing like the interior monologue of Molly Bloom or the stream of consciousness of Leopold Bloom, which are both full of incomplete sentences, disconcerting jumps and all sorts of odd bits and pieces of thought and perception.

## Irony

Irony is a technique of narration in fiction in which the narrator's tone suggests to the reader that he or she should not take what is said at face value, for the intended meaning may be the very opposite of what is apparently being said. In *Mrs Dalloway* irony is used as a means of satirising the manners, attitudes and beliefs of many of the characters, especially the minor characters. Since one of the main features of *Mrs Dalloway* is social satire, and in particular mockery of the decadent governing class in England at the time, it is not surprising that irony plays such a large role in the book. One of the ways a narrator can signal to the reader that a passage is to be read as ironical is to use deliberate exaggeration. For example, as the mysterious grey car carrying some very important but unidentified personage passes by, some of the men who see it 'perceived instinctively that greatness was passing, and the pale light of the immortal presence fell upon them as it had fallen upon Clarissa Dalloway' (page 18). The narrator is, of course, making fun of the idea that this mystery person might be a personification of greatness or could be immortal. The narrator, by the use of irony, conveys to the reader implicitly that the mystery person is more likely to be very ordinary indeed, just as is the Prime Minister who is treated with similar exaggerated respect when he turns up at Clarissa's party towards the end of the book.

Irony is to be found throughout *Mrs Dalloway*, but it is especially prominent whenever the narrator deals with Hugh Whitbread or Lady Bruton, characters who are clearly presented as particularly laughable. A signal that irony is involved is often given by the use of inflated description; words that are repeatedly used in this way are 'majestic' and 'magnificent', as for example when Lady Bruton is said to go 'ponderously, majestically, up to her room' (page 99) where she immediately falls asleep and snores upon her sofa. A parallel example in the case of

Hugh Whitbread is the description of him as 'a magnificent figure' as he inspects 'critically, magisterially' the shoes and socks in a shop window (page 92).

# Characters

Clarissa Dalloway's one gift is said to be that she knows people 'almost by instinct' (page 10); and yet she does not (in most cases) make judgements about them or attempt to sum them up. Peter Walsh is similarly hesitant, at least as far as Clarissa is concerned: 'It was a mere sketch, he often felt, that even he, after all these years, could make of Clarissa' (page 70). He is right, of course, and we should be careful in discussing the characters in the novel not to claim that we can do more than give sketches of them. Our knowledge of them is incomplete and many puzzles about them cannot be definitely settled. So we also must avoid saying 'they are this or they are that'. The reasons for this have been discussed above (in the section on 'Multiple points of view').

## The Dalloways

The objective facts about Clarissa Dalloway are that she is fifty-one years old and has recently suffered an illness which has turned her hair white. She is from a wealthy upper-class family and lives in some luxury in central London in a large house with many servants. Perhaps partly because of her illness and her sense of having aged, she seems preoccupied with death. But Peter Walsh remembers that even when she was young she had a horror of death and would have discussions about it with him. It may have been a decisive event in her life that as a young girl she witnessed the death of her sister who was killed accidentally, crushed by a falling tree. If Clarissa were to be judged harshly, there would be three main criticisms: her exaggerated need for security, her triviality and 'worldliness', and her frigidity, and these aspects of her character will be discussed in that order.

She is not a person who takes risks or is given to impulsive gestures. She is not adventurous. She needs security. There was a time when she was young when it still seemed possible that she might become different in these respects. She was in love with Sally Seton who was notoriously impulsive, a risk-taker. But Clarissa chose to marry Richard Dalloway rather than Peter Walsh. Richard was more steady and predictable, more competent and therefore comfortable, able to protect her against the shocks of life (as, for example, when her dog was injured, pages 67-8). Clarissa's own view of her choice of Richard puts it in a somewhat different light, for she does not think of it simply as a matter of having been feeble; she thinks of herself as vulnerable to disintegration. Without Richard's steadying and reliable presence she might not have been able to cope with the great terrors and panics from which she suffers. It is this which enables her to identify immediately with Septimus Warren Smith when she hears about his suicide (page 164) and this is something about her which has not been visible from the outside, even to those she has known well for many years.

Clarissa's choice of security is seen by Sally Seton negatively, as an incapacity. She thinks that Clarissa lacks something. Certainly, there are many ways in which Clarissa comes across as someone who lacks a great deal. She is a person of severe limitations. She is someone who can be seen to suffer from dreadful triviality. She takes no intelligent interest in politics, even though she lives at the centre of the political world. In fact, her ignorance seems to amuse her. That she tends to mix up Albanians and Armenians does not worry her one bit. In fact, we have no evidence that she has any serious interest in anything at all outside her social life and her daughter. Again, her own view of this seems rather complacent: 'She knew nothing; no language, no history; she scarcely read a book now, except memoirs in bed' (page 9). Perhaps, then, Miss Kilman's view of her is justified. Miss Kilman thinks that in spite of all her privileges she has frittered her life away in trivialities. 'She came from the most worthless of all classes – the rich with a smattering of culture' (page 110). The idea that she is no more than a snob receives some support even from Peter Walsh, for whom, 'the obvious thing to say of her was that she was worldly; cared too much for rank and society and getting on in the world' (page 69).

It is, however, quite possible for Clarissa to mount a defence against these charges (as she does, for example, on pages 108-9). Perhaps they are based on male prejudice, on men's inability to understand women's lives (Miss Kilman, as a modern, professional woman could be said to have absorbed male prejudices about traditional women's roles). Men like Peter Walsh value travel, love affairs, work, their careers. Other men admire dedication to country, and their heroes finish up as statues in the streets of London. Women's lives, in contrast, are obscure and unheroic and take place on the domestic, not on the public, stage. They cultivate children rather than Empires and who is to say that that is of lesser value? They build networks of caring relationships rather than networks of power and domination, and is this not just as admirable? Peter Walsh gives a very good sketch of this sort of women's activity (page 70): 'And behind it all was that network of visiting, leaving cards, being kind to people; running about with bunches of flowers, little presents . . . all that interminable traffic that women of her sort keep up.' As for her parties, they are, she thinks, 'an offering' (page 109), a notion that she finds difficult to spell out in words but which in any case she would not expect any man to understand.

One puzzle about Clarissa's life is her relationship with her daughter. When she feels challenged by Peter Walsh to account for her life (page 41), she lists Elizabeth as one of the central things in it; yet we do not in fact get much of a sense of any close involvement between them. Although Clarissa hates Miss Kilman for taking Elizabeth away from her, it is not at all clear that there was not already a distance between them quite independently of Miss Kilman's intervention. We do not, in any case, have any evidence that Clarissa makes sense of her life in terms of her having devoted it to bringing up Elizabeth. There is no evidence that she has found being a mother a fulfilling or satisfying role or that her relationship with Elizabeth is now of any great significance to her.

Clarissa Dalloway's other main characteristic is her emotional and physical frigidity. The words most often used about her are words such as 'cold', 'contracted', 'withdrawn', 'timid', 'wooden', 'rigid', 'unyielding' and 'impenetrable'. She is, says Walsh, 'as cold as an icicle' (page 72). She thinks of herself as like a nun, cloistered. She sometimes regrets that she lacks the warmth of physical intimacy, the fire of sexual passion. It is clear that she has suffered from sexual frigidity with her husband, that she somehow feels herself to have remained a virgin emotionally. She can suffer moments of regret if she thinks of her life as having been deprived of these consolations. Her single bed in the attic sums up her chilly existence: 'She had gone up into the tower alone and left them blackberrying in the sun' (page 43). Her brief experience of love with Sally Seton, culminating with her being kissed on the lips, and her occasional experience of desire for women, are described in terms of such rapturous and erotic warmth that there is no doubt that she knows just what she has missed (pages 30, 33).

There is, however, another way of seeing this. Clarissa's impenetrability may not be so entirely negative. If she is impenetrable, if she refuses to share and to be close beyond a certain point, this is not simply from fear, it is because she has a healthy resistance to the dependence of romantic love. She resists letting herself go, abandoning herself to passion, because she resists being taken over or dominated. She feels a strong need for privacy, independence, autonomy, even between husband and wife. Her fascination with the old woman in the house opposite seems to derive from this, that she is an image of privacy, of the distance that exists between people. Clarissa feels that intense emotions can be tyrannical. She thinks of both love and religion, the two intense emotional commitments in Miss Kilman's life, as being destructive and tyrannical forces. So although it is common in modern English culture to see resistance to ecstasy and abandonment as unhealthy, as a sign of neurotic repression of desire, there is a strong suggestion in *Mrs Dalloway* that there is another way of interpreting this resistance. It can be seen as an attempt to preserve some central core of identity from being forced or violated.

This resistance connects Mrs Dalloway to Septimus Warren Smith and gives her an instinctive understanding of his suicide. For she fears and distrusts Sir William Bradshaw and sees him as someone who would force or invade other people's souls. She can interpret Septimus's suicide, therefore, as a positive act of defiance and self-defence. She feels that the central core of individuality needs to be protected or it will be smashed by the philistines. She has within her, as Septimus had within him, some creative power, some vision, some poetry which they seek to destroy—it is noticeable that both she and Septimus draw comfort from their incantation of lines from Shakespeare, whereas Holmes tyrannically and Richard Dalloway priggishly will have nothing to do with him.

Elizabeth Dalloway provides a useful vantage point for discussing her mother's strengths and weaknesses. She is a pretty, seventeen-year-old girl. She is self-conscious and uncomfortable in public and feels that she would be happier in the country with her father and her dogs than in the city where people stare at her and admire her beauty. We do get a strong sense of the strength of attachment that there is between father and daughter, and this throws into relief the lack of evidence of any similar warmth or closeness between Elizabeth and her mother. She seems inclined to agree, at least in part, with Miss Kilman's assessment of her mother's life as trivial. She is in the process of rejecting her mother as a role model for her own life, and decides that she will not talk with her about this, which again suggests that they are not very close. She has been inspired by Miss Kilman's lessons on professions for women and wonders whether to be a farmer or a doctor. In any case, she would be unhappy in the traditional role of a woman of her class with her ambitions limited to marriage, children and parties. She is a modern girl and is being touched by some of the changes that have taken place in English society since the Great War. What this suggests to us is that the limitations of Clarissa's life are not to be understood entirely in terms of her individual psychology but that they to some extent derive from a framework of general social assumptions and constraints within which women of her generation were more or less trapped.

Richard Dalloway is also easiest to understand in terms of social categories. He is a typical land-owning gentleman. He has an estate in Norfolk and is addicted to country ways. He lives in London because of his dedication to public service as a Conservative Member of Parliament. He is not at all a figure of fun as is the pompous Hugh Whitbread. He seems to have generous, old-fashioned views about the poor. He is represented as altogether a decent but unexciting man who, like his wife, suffers from rather severe limitations. He is not in the front rank in politics and his career will go no higher. His achievements have been modest. He lacks imagination and political will. He cannot express his emotions: he is a typical English male, tongue-tied and inarticulate, who has to buy flowers for his wife because he is too shy to tell her that he loves her. But the warmth and tenderness of his feeling seem genuine, as does his attachment to his daughter.

## Sally Seton and Peter Walsh

Sally Seton is contrasted not only with Clarissa Dalloway but also with the Lady Rosseter that she later becomes. Her case reminds us that people do not necessarily have fixed, unchanging characters. As a girl she excited Clarissa and appalled her aunt with her unconventional behaviour. She was everything that Clarissa is not—impulsive, care-free, abandoned, unconventional, sexual. She was reckless. She could say anything to anyone. She was politically unconventional too, for she was a socialist, giving Clarissa the writings of William Morris and discussing with her plans for the abolition of private property. No doubt all this does have a certain charm, but we can quite understand how it might have irritated the adults and how her spontaneity might have been perceived by them as thoughtlessness (she left Clarissa's father's book out in the rain). In short, we can see from a different time perspective how all this youthful unconventionality was no more than immaturity and that it would not survive in the adult world. So it is not really a surprise when Sally Seton reappears transformed into Lady Rosseter, a complacent, self-satisfied mother of five boys with no surviving hint of radicalism or originality. She has married a million-aire and she sends her sons to Eton. She is thoroughly incorporated into the provincial, industrial bourgeoisie. There is no indication that she still reads or thinks. Her passion now, apart from her boys, is gar-dening.

Peter Walsh, of course, is most immediately contrasted with Richard Dalloway, since Clarissa chose between them. He is now fifty-two and everyone agrees that his life has been something of a failure. There is, people say, a flaw in his character so that he has always messed things up. He was expelled from the University of Oxford, he failed to marry Clarissa whom he loved, and he married on impulse on the boat on the way to India where he has followed an adequate, respectable but un-spectacular career in the Indian Civil Service. Now he is in love again, and this may be yet another of those mistakes which have dogged his life.

In spite of all this, there is undoubtedly something attractive about Peter Walsh, something that led Sally Seton to befriend him when they were young, and that has attracted women to him ever since. It is that he is not quite what a man was expected to be in ruling-class culture at that time. He is sceptical about male virtues and official values (he does not like army or Empire). He can see through the pretentious and pompous show put on by such people as Hugh Whitbread and the Prime Minister, and he is intolerant of humbug. He is not impressed by surface shows of magnificence, and that is why Clarissa's worldliness irritates him. He has a gentleman's manners—attentiveness and courtesy to women—and a certain gaiety. He is, unlike the self-conscious Richard Dalloway, openly emotional. He is given to confessing his private secrets. He bursts into tears when talking to Clarissa. He is, in short, 'not the sort of man one had to respect' (page 139). So if he is compared with the military man (like Daisy's husband) he would seem refreshing, alive. But contrasted with Dalloway he could seem weak and undisciplined.

There is then no single answer as to how to evaluate his unconventionality and his womanising. He had not the strength to overcome the troubles of the flesh, to discipline his body as a soldier would (page 47). But he has not the weakness to want to. We can understand why Clarissa is at one moment irritated by his 'silly unconventionality, his weakness' and yet the very next minute has kissed him and is saying to herself 'If I had married him, this gaiety would have been mine all day!' (pages 42-3). Clarissa has enjoyed a side of Peter that is not available to those who know him more distantly, for she has had a close and intimate relationship with him. But Peter could be suffocating; he could not tolerate that independence that she needed. Perhaps this inability to allow Clarissa her own space was his real weakness, that had spoiled his whole life, though it derived from the strength of his passion for her. He made demands on her (including, it is hinted, sexual demands) which she could not satisfy. He was jealous and possessive. He agrees in retrospect that his demands on her were absurd. There does seem to be something unattractively tense about him, some not quite healthy nervousness or aggression that shows itself in his playing with his pocket-knife, which both Clarissa and Sally know is a thing that he has done for thirty years.

## Miss Kilman

The portrait of Miss Kilman in *Mrs Dalloway* seems to be the product of an unrelenting and unswerving hatred. Unlike with the other characters, there is no ambiguity at all in her case. Even her name seems designed to sum her up in a word as a destructive force. We are familiar with the villains and heroes of popular literature having names that tell us who they are—Charles Dickens (1812-70), for example, often invented significant names for his characters. But this does not seem a good procedure for Virginia Woolf to adopt, in the context of her predominantly realist novel. It seems out of place, as though a character from a children's tale had got into the story by mistake. (Lady Bruton's name is another example in this novel: she is a brute and a Briton and her name invites us to laugh at her military pretensions and her exaggerated patriotism.)

Virginia Woolf's treatment of Miss Kilman may have been motivated by some private grudge or hatred. It is not at all clear why she felt the need to create such an utterly unappealing character and to express her own (and not just the characters') fierce revulsion for her, as if the very thought of her imagined body were unbearable. She is treated with such merciless contempt that the reader has to struggle to keep open any possibility of seeing her in any more generous or tolerant a spirit, with any degree of sympathy or pity. The only other character in this novel who receives this sort of treatment of authoritative denunciation is Sir William Bradshaw.

Miss Kilman's faults, as they are perceived by Mrs Dalloway, are love and religion. For her love is not disinterested love, but is a grasping, hungry, possessive kind of love that threatens Elizabeth's independence. It is associated symbolically with eating, as if she were longing to take Elizabeth into her mouth like cake. Her greed and her physical ugliness combine to give these passages of description an unpleasant power (page 117). The description really does make it seem that Elizabeth is in danger of being digested by some monstrous stomach.

Miss Kilman, except that she has the misfortune to come from a lower social class, is in some ways a parallel to Peter Walsh. For both of them the main problem is presented as being the desires of the body which resist or overturn discipline. 'It is the flesh', moans Miss Kilman (page 114), and she obviously does suffer enormously from the sheer power of her emotional drives. But whereas this is treated as a likeable unconventionality in Peter Walsh, it is treated ungenerously as a totally damning disease in Miss Kilman. Her religion, which she has, one might think wisely, adopted in an attempt to tame her emotional explosions of bitterness and self-disgust, seems like a genuine attempt to discover a solution to a real problem. As she prays in Westminster Abbey, she does seem to wage an authentic struggle against her agonies and a passer-by can see (as the narrator apparently cannot) something impressive in the physical energy with which she approaches her God (page 119).

To which one might add, if one were defending Miss Kilman against her detractor, the narrator, that she does seem to be of genuine benefit to Elizabeth. She is an intelligent, educated woman and an experienced teacher who has been able to arouse in Elizabeth (whose education seems otherwise to have been absurdly neglected, as was the fashion in that class) some intelligent interest in social problems, in history and in the position of women in society.

## Septimus and Lucrezia Warren Smith

Septimus Warren Smith's insanity is certainly based on Virginia Woolf's own experiences in 1895 and 1915. Most literary representations of madness are based on prejudice and stereotype and it is therefore of the greatest interest to have a character whose madness is described from the author's personal experience. Virginia Woolf also explores the problem in her other novels *The Voyage Out* and *The Waves*, but it is in Septimus Warren Smith that we have the fullest and most revealing account of the subjective experience of madness. It has been disputed whether it is right to use the word 'madness' at all, since this concept collects together under one heading such a very great variety of different forms of experience and different kinds of incapacity (such as lack of moral faculty, enfeebled intelligence, distorted perception, and so on). But 'madness' and 'insanity' are words that Virginia Woolf herself used often enough both in relation to herself and in relation to Septimus Warren Smith, and in *Mrs Dalloway* it is the doctor, Sir William Bradshaw, who refuses to use such words. He does this, however, not from any excess of sensitivity to his patients but because he refuses to take the problem of madness sufficiently seriously. He prefers to talk about people lacking a sense of proportion. Like the ignorant Dr Holmes, he wants to minimise the problem and to suggest that it results from some sort of moral failing in the patient.

Because the character of Septimus Warren Smith was conceived mainly as a vehicle for the representation of the subjective experience of mental disintegration, Virginia Woolf seems not to have had much interest in developing any other aspect of his personality. We are told very little about him or his background. In particular, we know next to nothing about his family. He is twenty-four years old, has been married for five years and seems to come from a lower-class background. He has managed to obtain some education and is of a literary turn of mind. Everything that is crucial to understanding his fate, however, has happened during and since the war. In the army he had been befriended by an officer called Evans, but he was killed just before the war ended. Psychologically the crucial aspect of this episode is Septimus's reaction to Evans's death: he could not grieve for him, and in fact seems to have repressed all feeling for him. It is this incapacity for feeling which worries and frightens him. He seems to experience even the most engaging things with detachment, as if at a distance. 'But beauty was behind a pane of glass' (page 79). He can no longer engage properly with the world. Septimus himself comes to regard his inability to feel grief for Evans's death as an unforgivable crime and he becomes at times overwhelmed with guilt because of it.

Septimus's mental state was not completely incapacitating in the first years after the war. He married Lucrezia, a hat-maker, daughter of an innkeeper in Milan. She is a likeable, simple woman whose main ambition is to have children and who is manifestly out of her depth with Septimus's illness. She does not understand at all what is happening to him and is at first inclined to believe the ludicrous Dr Holmes, for whom mental disintegration and suicidal depression are no more than forms of cowardice to be cured by a stern moral lecture. In fact we have in the character of Septimus a very full and complex portrait of insanity, with a very subtle rendering of a whole range of symptoms. The representation of insanity is discussed fully in a separate section below.

The problem about the character of Septimus Warren Smith that needs to be discussed here is that of his role in the novel. The novel was originally conceived as a study of the personality of the society hostess and of 'party consciousness'. Onto this was grafted the utterly different theme of madness and the completely unconnected story of Septimus Warren Smith. What sort of relation between these two totally different stories did Virginia Woolf want to achieve? She was worried that this apparently quite arbitrary gluing together of unconnected parts would be picked on by the critics. She wrote in her diary (13 December 1924): 'The reviewers will say that it is disjointed because of the mad scenes not connecting with the Dalloway scenes.' If it is not disjointed, what kind of joins are there between the stories? Clarissa Dalloway and the Warren Smiths never meet. They come from quite different parts of society. The connections between them at the level of plot are completely accidental. They are all three in Bond Street at the same time. Later, Peter Walsh happens by chance to walk past the Warren Smiths in Regent's Park. Elizabeth Dalloway happens by chance to pass by somewhere in the vicinity of their home on a bus in the afternoon. The only person who actually meets both Clarissa and Septimus is Sir William Bradshaw, and it is through the coincidence of his attending her party on the day of Septimus's suicide that Clarissa happens to get to hear of his death. So at this level, of connections between the lives of the two characters, there is nothing but chance. What then did Virginia Woolf mean when she said in an Introduction to the American edition of *Mrs Dalloway* that 'in the first version Septimus, who later is intended to be her double, had no existence; . . . Mrs Dalloway was originally to kill herself, or perhaps merely to die at the end of the party'?

One thing that she might have meant was simply that she was interested in comparing sanity with insanity and that this is made less abstract if you have two characters, one sane and the other insane, reacting simultaneously to the very same events in the world. She wrote in her diary (14 October 1922) that 'I adumbrate here a study of insanity and suicide; the world seen by the sane and the insane, side by side'. It is true that the study of insanity is immensely enriched by this method (see the discussion below), but it is not true that this comparison of the reactions of the sane and the insane is always a comparison between Clarissa and Septimus. Septimus's reactions to events in the world are compared with those of many other characters and only very occasionally with Clarissa's. So this cannot be the sense in which Septimus is her double. But there is one particular thing with which they are both preoccupied and which connects them together very strongly at the level of a common theme, and that is death. Clarissa's life has been lived under the shadow of her sister's death and Septimus's life has been decisively interrupted by the death of Evans. They are both thinking a great deal about death on the day of the action of the novel, so it could be argued that they do present interesting similarities and differences in their views and reactions to death and their different capacities for coping with it.

Clarissa and Septimus both struggle to make sense of death, to find a way of thinking about it. When she was young Clarissa thought up theories about death which are remembered by Peter Walsh. As a young girl she had explained that she felt herself to be everywhere: we are not just the person that is visible, for that is only the superficial part of ourselves. There is also an unseen part of ourselves, and this part is everywhere, spread out amongst all the things that we see and touch and places that we know. This dispersed part of ourselves can be attached to other people, even to people we have never spoken to and, she thought, it might survive 'somehow attached to this person or that, or even haunting certain places, after death' (page 136). This is, of course, exactly the kind of relationship that Clarissa has with Septimus, to whom she has never spoken and who strangely seems to haunt her briefly, or achieve some communication with her briefly, after his death. When she hears of his death it is as if Septimus's unseen self has spread across London and into her room where he survives as an influence on her.

The fifty-one-year old Clarissa's thoughts about death do not seem to be very different from those she had as a young girl. We learn of them very early in the book, for as she walks towards Bond Street she asks herself 'did it matter that she must inevitably cease completely . . . or did it not become consoling to believe that death ended absolutely?' (page 10). But she still believes that something survives, spread out like a mist in the trees, touching even 'people she had never met'. What matters to her most now, it seems, is to maintain her courage in the face of death, to not be defeated by it. Everybody has had a great deal of practice in doing that in recent years because of the war so that they had all to learn courage, to be stoical.

Septimus, of course, has been broken by his experience of the war and of Evans's death. Given the atrocious conditions and the monstrous waste of human life in the trenches of the First World War it is almost inconceivable that anyone could have survived it without being in some way deeply damaged. Septimus's restless, creative mind searches for explanations and hunts for meanings, but it is one of the symptoms of his madness that he cannot sustain a belief in any of his visions or interpretations for very long. He swings wildly from his glorious visions of the dead surviving in paradise to a state of utter despair. One minute he has a great revelation that there is no death, at another moment he believes that 'it might be possible that the world itself is without meaning' (page 79). So Septimus is Clarissa's double in that he is a picture of what happens if the precarious balance of sanity is dislodged. For sanity is not portrayed in Clarissa as a stable, rock-like condition that cannot be shifted by the accidents of a life. It is rather the ability to maintain a mask of gaiety and unconcern; it is retaining the capacity to assemble oneself into a public person even when hurt inside. (Clarissa's heroine is Lady Bexborough who opened a bazaar while holding in her hand the telegram announcing that her son had been killed in the war.) Sanity is having the spirit to decorate the prison we are all in with flowers (page 70), as Septimus in a brief period of normality shortly before his death helps Rezia to decorate a hat with flowers. Clarissa suffers, like Septimus, from a tendency to sudden and irrational panics and she knows that the distance that separates sanity from insanity is a narrow one. This is why she can instantly recognise her kinship with Septimus even though she has never met him: 'Then (she had felt it only this morning) there was the terror; the overwhelming incapacity ... there was in the depths of her heart an awful fear ... She had escaped. But that young man had killed himself' (page 164). Madness and suicide have been real, potential futures for them both.

The closest Septimus comes to being Clarissa's double is in their common experiences of tranquility, of release from pressure, which are described in each case in almost identical terms. Clarissa's moment of peace comes in the morning, as she sits on her sofa mending her green dress (pages 36-7). Septimus's moment of peace comes shortly before his death. He also is on a sofa resting; he is watching the play of light on the walls (page 124). This shared vision does suggest some kind of closeness or likeness between Clarissa and Septimus, some connection between the invisible deeper parts of themselves, that legitimates Clarissa's saying that 'she felt somehow very like him – the young man who had killed himself' (page 165).

# Themes

## War and Empire

The reaction of society to the unprecedented experience of the Great War is a theme which runs throughout *Mrs Dalloway*. Many of the characters' lives have been influenced by the war directly or indirectly, most obviously, of course, that of Septimus Warren Smith. His reactions to the war can be taken as a metaphor for the general reaction of the ruling stratum of society as a whole. The notable thing about his experience was that after the end of the war he carried on apparently unchanged by it, with no observable damage. It was only several years later that the deep inner injuries that he had suffered began to affect his overt behaviour, until a point was reached where he could no longer carry on at all. This delayed reaction, the apparent absorption of the experience without injury for years after the war was over, seems to have been, on Virginia Woolf's view, the reaction of society at large. The action of the novel takes place in 1923, five years after the end of the war, and there are many signs that its significance has not yet been understood, its impact not yet fully appreciated.

The ruling class are portrayed by Virginia Woolf as living in a state of disguised decadence. They have carried on as though the war has taught them nothing. They have no notion that the war was a decisive experience in English, and more generally European, culture, and that all the old assumptions which formed the foundations of the social and political order, should no longer remain unquestioned. Their reaction has been delayed. Although there have been the beginnings of change at the level of personal behaviour, especially in relation to the public appearance and behaviour of women (and Peter Walsh notes these changes with approval) there is still a general cultural immobility among what Walsh calls 'the governing class'.

Lady Bruton is the most striking representative of this class. Coming from a powerful military family, she fails to respond intelligently to what is happening in the world. Like most members of her class, for example, she is horrified by what is happening in India where there are the beginnings of a challenge to the British imperial pretensions and the demand for independence. Her values are traditional. In fact, she is a very good personification of tradition. It is not just a matter of ideas being made familiar by virtue of having been around a long time. Tradition exists more deeply – it affects values, the sense of family, even of personal identity, and as we can see in Lady Bruton's case, even the physical postures of those who live within it. The traditions to which she belongs are archaic military and imperial traditions that are now irreversibly out of date. Virginia Woolf makes fun of her long family line of army generals stretching back behind her. It is notable that the forms of warfare at which they excelled and which Lady Bruton would herself like to have carried on are old-fashioned, primitive forms which have no place in the twentieth century. She sees herself as a general of dragoons, that is, as a leader of glamorous cavalry troops who did their fighting on horseback and excelled through personal skills with archaic weapons. There were cavalry soldiers in the First World War, but their era was already really in the past. Modern war was a matter of mud and trenches, machine guns and tanks and even the beginnings of aerial bombardment. In this context, the vision of Lady Bruton with helmet, arrow and shield (page 160) is definitely ludicrous.

Richard Dalloway, who is not, on the whole, treated unkindly in the novel, is, however, exposed as a bit of a fool when it comes to his attitudes to Lady Bruton. For he himself is rather seduced by the traditions which she represents, and by the myths of the great military families (the very people who had proved themselves as a class to be murderously incompetent in their conduct of the war). For he plans to write a history of her family, respecting as he does their values and achievements, even though Lady Bruton herself is manifestly a simple-minded philistine (of 'downright feelings, and little introspective power' (page 97) says the generous narrator).

Lady Bruton also suffers from an associated distortion of values in that she is a great believer in patriotism, this being a value which Virginia Woolf throughout her life regarded with contempt. Patriotism amounts to an uncritical, unthinking loyalty to one's country and it was just this attitude ('my country right or wrong' as people said) that had taken the nations of Europe into the most dreadful and bloody war. It is in fierce satiric tone that it is said of Lady Bruton that one could not imagine her even after death being parted from English soil 'or roaming territories over which, in some spiritual shape, the Union Jack had ceased to fly. To be not English even among the dead—no, no! Impossible!' (page 160). At this time, the protracted disintegration of the British Empire was about to begin, but to those who ruled it, this was inconceivable. The Empire at that time included a quarter of the entire population of the earth and on it, it was said, the sun never set.

Peter Walsh offers the best contrast to Lady Bruton in his attitudes to war and empire, both of which he dislikes. Seeing boys marching through London in military formation, among the statues of great military heroes, reminds him that he was brought up as a boy to worship these dead soldiers and to see history as the story of famous battles which they won. There is no doubt that his rejection of these models for his life is among the characteristics that make him seem a failure in the eyes of the powerful. His own rejection of military virtues is confirmed when he contemplates the passing parade, which is described in a witty ironical image (pages 46-7). The attitudes and stiff machine-like movements of the boys are inculcated by military discipline and this is associated with death. It is as if they have to die in order to become soldiers.

Peter Walsh has never been willing to give up his warm, sexual body in order to become a cold military machine nor to give up his individuality in order to become incorporated into this collective unit.

So a general theme of the book is that traditional culture (or at least traditional male culture) denies the reality of war by covering it with images of glamour and heroism. It also links it with other archaic, sentimental images, notably with those associated with royalty. A good example of this is Mr Bowley who is said to be 'sealed with wax over the deeper sources of life' (page 19), which is to say that he is unable to feel any authentic, vital emotions for they are so strongly repressed. Yet tears come to his eyes as he contemplates widows and children and thinks about the war as the mystery car, carrying perhaps a royal person, passes by. What he seems to feel is sentimental pride: 'A breeze flaunting ever so warmly . . . past the bronze heroes, lifted some flag flying in the British breast of Mr Bowley' (page 19). A question the novel seems implicitly to ask is, which is more truly the death of the soul, that of a woman who lives a trivial life as a hostess (for Peter Walsh says that Clarissa suffers from a death of the soul) or that of men who are incapable of feeling except for a sentimental patriotic pride and attachment to images of warfare and royalty.

## Power

Power is another theme in relation to which we know from other evidence that the anger expressed by the narrator of *Mrs Dalloway* is Virginia Woolf's own. The section of the novel most obviously focused on this theme is that in which Sir William Bradshaw is attacked for being a worshipper of the Goddess Conversion (pages 88-91). On the face of it, it is not at all clear that the attack on Bradshaw is justified. He is a professional medical man performing his job within the limitations imposed upon him by the lack of medical knowledge of mental disease in his day. Septimus clearly is seriously incapacitated when he goes for his consultation with Bradshaw; he has been suicidal, and he has been making his wife's life a misery with fear. He does need help. The dreadful Dr Holmes, who is an ignorant, insensitive and arrogant fool, has been of no use whatsoever. Bradshaw is surely a great improvement. He immediately recognises that Septimus is very ill. There is nothing obviously cruel or outrageous in his recommendation that Septimus go into a home where he can be properly cared for. In the absence of modern drugs, and given that it was in the very early days of the psychoanalytic movement, it is not easy to see what else could be done to help someone unfortunate enough to suffer from severe mental derangement.

The anger of the narrator and the ironic description of Bradshaw as a worshipper of the Goddess Conversion are based on the accusation that there is something illegitimate about the manner in which he wields power. Clarissa Dalloway's instinctive dislike of Bradshaw is based on the same intuition about him. In her mind he is 'obscurely evil . . . capable of some indescribable outrage—forcing your soul, that was it' (page 163). In Clarissa's mind this outrage, 'forcing your soul', is what is involved in any attempt by one person to impose their will on another. For example, it is also involved in that pair of negative passions from which the unfortunate Miss Kilman suffers—love and religion. For these all involve one person trying to subdue another so that they lose their independence, dominating them so strongly that they lose their own will-power. In Bradshaw's case, it is said, he has not only imposed his will in this way on his patients but also on his wife, who fifteen years ago 'had gone under': her will had slowly sunk into his (page 90).

In relation to his patients, Bradshaw's position is even more horrendous: with them (if they have ever threatened to kill themselves) all resistance or opposition is useless. Bradshaw has not only his wealth and social position, not only his being a man and a professional expert, to call upon to support his attack upon his patient's will—he can also call upon the law. The law puts him in a position of making judgements about his patients—this one is sane, that insane, this one can have children, that one not, this one must be locked up while that one can go free for now. This legal power sweeps away all resistance. Of course, Bradshaw can convince himself that his reasons for exercising power over people's lives are most respectable: he is protecting society, he is upholding noble values, love, duty, self-sacrifice. But, it is suggested, his motives are less acceptable: he lusts for power, he hungers to convert others to his bidding, he thrills at his control over other people's lives. And so he locks them up, forbids them to see their friends, tells them what to eat. In these passages Virginia Woolf is clearly expressing her own sense of outrage at the violence done to her in the name of medicine when she was herself put away in a nursing home, prevented from seeing her friends and forced to eat cream and eggs which she loathed. She is clearly on the side of those patients who call Bradshaw 'a damnable humbug' (page 91). She thinks of him as a fraud and a hypocrite. He claims that his power is based on knowledge and understanding, but she knows very well that it is not, for he does not understand Septimus, does not listen to him, has no idea at all of the meaning of anything he says or of the origin of his distress. She was surely right that doctors at that time had little understanding of mental illness and that those who put on a show of professional certainty and confidence in their judgements about it were mere impostors.

## Madness

Virginia Woolf said in her diary (14 October 1922) that *Mrs Dalloway* would contain a study of 'the world seen by the sane and the insane, side by side'. This comparison allows us to see the similarities and differences that there are between the mental processes of the sane and the insane, in Virginia Woolf's view of the matter. The striking conclusion we can draw is that in the novel the mental processes of those whom we recognise to be disturbed are not fundamentally different from those of the 'healthy' or 'normal' characters. It is certainly true that Septimus Warren Smith is represented as having crossed some line into a state of incapacitating distress and madness, but the workings of his mind are like an exaggerated version of those of other people and are not fundamentally different. For example, we have already commented above that he is not the only character to suffer from sudden, severe panic attacks, for Mrs Dalloway also suffers from these. Similarly, his emotional reactions are clearly sometimes inappropriate and abnormally intense in the circumstances; but so are those of Mr Bowley, Miss Kilman and Peter Walsh. Distortion of the emotional life of one kind or another is represented as being a general feature of English society and not in itself a symptom of insanity. Septimus suffers from a disabling degree of something that in itself is perceived as normal.

This same general relationship between the 'sane' and the 'insane' can be seen in many other examples. Septimus is given to the 'insane' habit of looking for signs and messages in the events of the world around him. When he sees the plane flying over London sky-writing, he misinterprets what it is doing, for he believes it to be writing a personal message for himself. This is where his madness lies. But he is by no means the only character who is looking for a message or a revelation. His interpretation of the sky-writing is like a parody of a normal activity of the mind. Look at the reactions to it of Mr Bentley, for example: he sees the plane as 'a symbol . . . of man's soul; of his determination . . . to get outside his body, beyond his house, by means of thought' (pages 26-7). The joke, of course, is that the plane's message is completely banal, being merely an advertisement for toffee. But such is the need of the human mind for meaning, that many fall into the temptation to read into it something more grandly significant.

Taking things as symbols is a symptom of this human desire for meaning. It is, of course, quite normal, though it tends to be more common in some people than in others. Sir William Bradshaw catches

Septimus 'attaching meanings to words of a symbolical kind' (page 86) and pronounces this a serious symptom of madness. But we can all see things not just as what they are but as what they remind us of or are associated with in our minds. The novel makes fun of people's tendency to see Elizabeth Dalloway not as the shy young adolescent that she is but as a tree, an animal or a flower (page 119). Sally Seton says that Elizabeth looks like 'a lily by the side of a pool' (page 171); Virginia Woolf is surely underlining a similarity between Septimus's mind and Sally's mind when she has Septimus say that Rezia 'looked pale, mysterious, liké a lily, drowned, under water' (page 80). Of course, Septimus goes further than this; he tends to take things for other than they are literally rather than metaphorically. He takes Peter Walsh to be his friend Evans; he takes a motor horn to be heavenly music. This visionary transformation of experience is a negative and destructive force for Septimus because it is accompanied by intolerable emotions of guilt, anxiety or fear, and because he becomes so utterly absorbed in his visions that he loses touch with reality.

The same argument could be put forward in relation to Septimus's other symptoms. For example, he suffers from extreme swings of mood, from wild exultation to blackest despair, from excitable engagement to extreme detachment. These swings, though extreme, are not fundamentally different from those suffered during the day by Peter Walsh or by Clarissa Dalloway. Or consider Septimus's attitude to sex ('Love between man and woman was repulsive... The business of copulation was filth', page 80). This is not totally dissimilar to Clarissa's frigidity, her distaste for physical love between man and woman. So although the book does not at all minimise the extent to which Septimus is disturbed and distressed, the presentation of his condition does seem to focus on and emphasise the similarity between his mental processes and those of the other characters. These processes are the normal ones, but in Septimus's case they seem to have become unchained from the perception of reality and uncontrolled by the demands of practical life so that they operate beyond the normal bounds.

## Time

An early version of *Mrs Dalloway* was called 'The Hours' and this serves to remind us that time is a central theme in the novel. Perhaps it is more accurate to say that the theme is the existence of different time frameworks. The first of these is the framework of objective or *clock time*. Throughout the novel the subjective lives of the characters are interrupted by reminders of the regular and inexorable passage of objective time, signalled by the striking of clocks. The framework of clock time does, of course, have a certain usefulness. It helps the various characters to integrate their social lives and their collective activities; or to put it more simply, it allows them to fix and keep appointments for lunch or with their doctors. But it is also, being impersonal, a constant background reminder of the material world and its inhuman processes which go on endlessly regardless of human desires. The chiming of the clocks is sometimes announced by a repeated refrain, which points up this message: 'First a warning, musical; then the hour, irrevocable. The leaden circles dissolved in the air' (page 6). The vibrations of clock time die away rapidly in the air. They are heavily material, leaden, and have little power to remain alive.

In sharp contrast to this is the framework of *subjective time*. Subjective moments are preserved in memory and do not die away rapidly. Remembered moments are recalled (called back again), though of course they cannot be relived. Not all past moments are of equal significance. Subjective time, unlike clock time, does not flow evenly and is not marked by regular divisions. Events or experiences which turn out to be particularly crucial or memorable do not occur predictably. Clarissa and her friends all see that summer long ago at Bourton as having been crucial in determining their whole lives and they each have vivid memories of it. For Septimus it has turned out that the death of his friend Evans is an event which has subsequently dominated his subjective life: it is as if subjectively he cannot go beyond it, as if his subjective time has become frozen at that point so that he lives it over and over again in various guises.

A particularly fine description of the operation of subjective time is to be found when Elizabeth Dalloway is thinking about her future (page 122), (for subjective time can make present the future as well as the past). At the end of the passage Elizabeth is recalled to the practical, social life and for that the framework she needs to consult is that of clock time, so she must shift from one framework to the other.

This is a crucial moment for Elizabeth and its effects may vibrate for ever down the years of her life. Moments like this happen to many of the characters and are commonly signalled, as here, by the word 'revelation'. It is often not at all clear, even to those whose experiences they are, just what it is that marks them off as out of the ordinary. Look, for example, at Peter Walsh: 'He had found life like an unknown garden, full of turns and corners, surprising, yes; really it took one's breath away, these moments . . . [like this] moment, in which things came together; this ambulance; and life and death' (page 135). Or look at Clarissa: 'Only for a moment, she had seen an illumination; a match burning in a crocus; an inner meaning almost expressed' (page 30). These fleeting experiences of revelation confirm that we live our lives in different time frameworks—a practical time in which we are busy and active and engaged with things in the world, and some other kind of time in which a meaning of a deeper, more enduring kind shines briefly through. The meaning of these moments is not expressed in words. Virginia Woolf does not offer any philosophical or religious interpretation of them. But the idea of special moments recurs in many of her works. Sometimes she calls them 'moments of vision' (after a poem with that title by Thomas Hardy, English poet and novelist, 1840-1928). In the last year of her life she wrote a sketch for an autobiography in which she called them 'moments of being': her autobiographical writings were later collected together and published under that title.

A third framework is that of *historical time*. This is the framework we use when we give meaning to the history of our nations or societies, for we mark out their past into different epochs or see it as marked out by particularly significant historical events (as for example when Christian cultures measure time by reference to the birth of Christ, or when we label an epoch 'the Renaissance' or refer to a decisive period as that of the Industrial Revolution). In *Mrs Dalloway* there is a constant background assumption that a great and decisive discontinuity in historical time had recently occurred, an event of such magnitude that it will later be seen as 'epoch-making'. This was the Great War. Most of the 'governing class' do not seem to be aware of the crucial significance of this historical event: it is as if society and culture had not yet caught up with what had happened.

Historical time tends in our culture to be structured around *men's* activities (kings, wars, parliaments) and in *Mrs Dalloway* we see society reminded of it mainly in the commemorative monuments which are scattered throughout the city. They mostly celebrate wars and their heroes. The assumption that is reflected in this fact is that it is these male activities which have historical value. Women's lives, which are domestic and not public, do not, in this view, contribute to historical time. Virginia Woolf herself disagreed strongly with this assumption, for she felt that the creativity of women's lives as expressed in the domestic sphere makes an essential contribution to holding societies together and moving forward in historical time. In *Mrs Dalloway* the narrow male view of history is made fun of (see the section on 'War and Empire', above).

Beyond historical time there is yet another time framework, which we may call evolutionary or *cosmic time*. This is a time framework which had become of great importance in English culture since the publication of Darwin's theory of evolution in the mid-nineteenth century, and Clarissa is herself familiar with it from her reading of Huxley and Tyndall. It is the framework of the time of the universe and its evolution, far greater expanses of time than those of human history.

Viewing human lives and human history in the perspective of this time framework had greatly contributed to the erosion of religious belief (as, it seems, in Clarissa Dalloway's case) in English culture. We get a brief and comic glimpse of this cosmic perspective in *Mrs Dalloway* in the figure of an old beggar-woman who sings in the street outside Regent's Park. She sings a song as old as the time before human life began, when the earth was covered with swamps where mammoths roamed, a song of the millions of years of human history which pass so swiftly, and of the time when human history will come to an end and the earth will be covered in ice. In this framework, death is victorious. 'Death's enormous sickle had swept those tremendous hills' and 'the passing generations . . . vanished, like leaves, to be trodden under, to be soaked and steeped and made mould of by that eternal spring' (pages 73-4).

It is a comic vision, this poor and wretched woman singing of such tremendous themes as the passage of infinite ages and the death of the earth. But it would be a mistake to read into this image some solemn or cosmic meaning that Virginia Woolf is trying to present as the meaning of her novel. This would be to repeat Septimus's mistake of misreading messages. Just as the sky-writing does turn out to be legible but not to be a revelation, so this woman's singing, a 'frail quivering sound . . . with an absence of all human meaning' (pages 72-3) as Peter Walsh first thinks when he hears it, turns out to be an intelligible song. We can understand what the woman is singing about without jumping to the conclusion that Virginia Woolf has put her there to provide the reader with a revelation, a key which will unlock the secrets of all the rest of the novel. It provides one more perspective to be added to all the other points of view. It also provides us with an image of *Mrs Dalloway* itself. The novel, on first reading, can disappoint our expectations, if we have been hoping for a dramatic story or some final message. It can seem a thin and insubstantial sound. Reading the book patiently, we do not come upon a hidden meaning, but we increasingly become familiar with its multiple themes and multiple points of view and increasingly satisfied with its song-like qualities, its rhythms and refrains.

# Part 4

# Hints for study

## The main problems in studying *Mrs Dalloway*

*Mrs Dalloway* is not constructed in the same way as many more familiar novels. Earlier sections of these Notes have examined the ways in which *Mrs Dalloway* is unusual in its methods of characterisation, in the form of its plot and story and in its narrative techniques. These features of the book can be expected not only to create problems for the student who is not used to dealing with novels of this kind, but also to appeal to the examiner who is trying to design examination questions so as to find out whether the candidates have succeeded in understanding the book. Usually, when reading a novel, the reader organises his or her memory of the book around the progress of the story. If the reader then wants to look something up, he or she can hope to find it by remembering with which episodes in the story it is associated. Similarly, the reader tends to organise knowledge of character around particular actions, events or decisions, and these can often be located in the story. With *Mrs Dalloway* these intuitive ways of familiarising oneself with a novel are less available than usual because the narration does not follow a continuous story; it shifts from one character to another and it jumps backwards and forwards in time from present to past and (occasionally) future.

A good way of overcoming these difficulties and of getting a clear grasp of the main structures of the book is to construct a simple chart of the book's most important shifts as it is read through (but *not* as it is read through for the first time). It is best to base the chart on the book's two main structural features, which are: (i) the objective passage of time through the day and (ii) the subjective shifts from one character's point of view to another. Read through the book noting down carefully each time the reader is given information about either the time of day or a shift in the point of view. The time of day is given by the narrator mentioning the chiming of clocks; it is not always specified what time it is when the clocks chime, but this can gradually be worked out. To the chart can be added, of course, selected information about the events, encounters and memories of the characters. The idea is that the chart should replace the usual methods of making notes on reading through the book. Page 57 gives a small sample of how the information can be set out.

| Page | Time | Character | Notes |
| --- | --- | --- | --- |
| 53-59 | | Peter Walsh | he remembers Bourton; 'death of the soul', Clarissa's coldness—she will be a perfect hostess; Clarissa rejects him |
| 59 | | Lucrezia | agony and self-pity |
| 61 | | Septimus | hallucinates about Evans; a great revelation |
| 64 | 11.45 | Peter Walsh | he sees the Warren Smiths; how society has changed since the war |

Obviously, the notes collected in the right-hand column can become more and more elaborate as the reader becomes more familiar with the book and wants to note a greater variety of information.

## Refrains and keywords

It could be very useful to add to the chart a fifth column on the right-hand side labelled 'Refrains and keywords'. In this column the student could note two things. First he or she could note occurrences of the little refrains that are repeated through the book. Note the quotation from Shakespeare's *Cymbeline*, 'Fear no more the heat o' the sun' (which sometimes appears just as 'Fear no more'). Then note the little refrain that sometimes accompanies the striking of the clock (and again the whole refrain is not always used), 'First the warning, musical; then the hour, irrevocable. The leaden circles dissolved in the air' (page 6). It is also worth noting repetitions of the phrase, 'That is all'.

It is often said that Virginia Woolf is a poetic writer and one aspect of her writing is the fact that she likes to repeat poetic refrains in this way. This is one more way in which her work is rather different from traditional fiction. These refrains have several functions: the quotation from *Cymbeline* is one of the ways in which the narration establishes a connection between Clarissa and Septimus even though they never meet and do not know each other. The fact that it is repeated keeps before the reader's mind the fact that underneath the surface chatter and movement of the novel there is a serious purpose which keeps breaking through, and that is to represent the way in which some of the characters are privately preoccupied with death. It is notable that when they are calmed and freed from their terror it is not by means of some theory nor by some religious belief about death, but by means of a song. The function of the second refrain is not totally unconnected with this, for it is a poetic statement that keeps breaking through, with the signalling of the passage of impersonal time, of the differences between that time and the time of individual consciousness which is the uneven time of activity, memory and desire.

Repeated 'keywords' are another aspect of Virginia Woolf's poetic technique. In *Mrs Dalloway* she does not always present her themes directly and explicitly. For example, there is a great deal of comment in the novel about war, both about the First World War and about war in general. But we are not given straightforward discussion or arguments about war. We do not find characters presenting different points of view on war explicitly. Rather, comment about war is to be found implicitly in the way things are described or in the sorts of images that characters or the narrator use. Examples of this are the satirical descriptions of Lady Bruton in terms of her military bearing, or in Peter Walsh's memories of having General Gordon as a hero when he was a boy. There is particularly powerful imagery associated with war in the section in which Peter Walsh watches a parade of uniformed boys march up Whitehall (page 47). For here a very clear attitude to war is endorsed without any explicit argument, the attitude being based on the connection that is established by the imagery between military discipline and death: the discipline of the march is repeatedly connected with wreaths, corpses and the immobility of statues. As another example, consider the way the falsity of patriotism as an emotion is asserted by the use of the image of Mr Bowley being 'sealed with wax over the deeper sources of life'. Or think about how Clarissa's frigidity is established by references to her being 'cloistered' and like a nun. The chart can be quite a useful way of collecting and retrieving information about striking imagery in the text.

As the student becomes more familiar with the text, he or she should find that more and more thematically significant keywords and images will suggest themselves for listing on the chart, so that the variety of their uses can be studied efficiently and so that good illustrative quotations can be located quickly. As an example, one might consider listing all the uses of what could be called mock heroic or mock stately descriptions which involve such words as 'magnificent', 'magisterial', or 'majestic', in this way building up a good picture of how satire is used in the book, especially in the mockery of Hugh Whitbread, Lady Bruton and the Prime Minister. Another useful exercise would be to chart all the words which are applied to Clarissa to suggest her frigidity, words such as 'cold', 'rigid', 'petrified', 'contracted', and so on.

Perhaps most useful of all as a learning exercise, and one that can take a student close to the heart of the book's main themes, is to list all the uses of the word 'revelation' or associated words referring to special moments of illumination. Virginia Woolf does not put forward a theory or philosophy concerning revelations; she simply acquaints us with a great variety of experiences of revelatory moments so that we can judge for ourselves what to make of them. Some of these revelations are insane. For example, Septimus thinks: 'Men must not cut down trees. There is a God. (He noted such *revelations* on the backs of envelopes.)' (page 23). On another occasion, when Septimus is alone at home, he thinks for the first time that he can hear the voice of his dead friend Evans: 'It was at that moment (Rezia had gone shopping) that the great *revelation* took place. A voice spoke from behind the screen. Evans was speaking. The dead were with him' (page 83). In contrast, some of Clarissa's moments of revelation are erotic: when kissed by Sally, Clarissa felt 'the radiance burnt through, the *revelation*, the religious feeling!' (page 33). In the case of Peter Walsh, the word revelation refers to something quite different, to moments of psychological insight, as for example the moment when he realised that Clarissa would marry Richard Dalloway: 'He was a prey to *revelations* at that time. This one—that she would marry Dalloway—was blinding—overwhelming at the moment' (page 56). Such significant moments of insight or strong feeling are not always referred to as revelations. It would be worth including on the chart a reference to such moments as Peter Walsh's rather mysterious moment of vision outside the British Museum (page 135), and perhaps Richard Dalloway's feeling that his life has been a miracle (page 103).

As we read through the book we find that the words referring to this range of illuminating experiences ring like bells and vibrate in our minds as a pebble sends off ripples when thrown into water.

## Specimen questions*

(1) Mrs Dalloway does not tell an exciting story and yet the reader's interest is engaged throughout. Do you agree?

(2) *Mrs Dalloway* combines the story of Clarissa Dalloway's party with that of Septimus Warren Smith's suicide. How are these different stories integrated in the novel?

(3) Is there anything distinctive about the role of the narrator in *Mrs Dalloway*?

---

* The author owes his thanks to Mary Sabine-Bacon of Kingsway-Princeton College for help with these questions.

(4) Virginia Woolf said that in *Mrs Dalloway* she described 'the world seen by the sane and the insane side by side'. What do we learn from the comparison?

(5) Is *Mrs Dalloway* convincing as the representation of the inner life of Clarissa Dalloway or Peter Walsh or Lucrezia Warren Smith?

(6) In *Mrs Dalloway* are there any interesting contrasts between the male and female characters?

(7) '*Mrs Dalloway* presents a satirical view of society.' Discuss.

(8) 'Clarissa Dalloway is no more than a trivial, superficial snob.' Discuss.

(9) 'Death of the soul', thinks Peter Walsh about Clarissa Dalloway. Is he right?

(10) Discuss the representation of memory and its role in subjective life in *Mrs Dalloway*.

(11) Compare and contrast the structure of *Mrs Dalloway* with that of any other novel of your choice.

(12) Why do clocks chime throughout *Mrs Dalloway*?

(13) Is Virginia Woolf successful in evoking London and its life in *Mrs Dalloway*?

(14) When Clarissa hears of Septimus's suicide, 'she felt glad that he had done it'. Why?

(15) '*Mrs Dalloway* is a celebration of life.' Is it?

## Problems of ambiguity

The central subject of the novel is the character of Mrs Dalloway herself. The reader might feel that he or she should finish the book with a clear idea of who Mrs Dalloway is. In fact, as has been emphasised elsewhere in these Notes, there are many important points on which one feels unsure still at the end of the book. There are points about Mrs Dalloway's character which remain uncertain or ambiguous. This is reflected in critical commentaries on the novel. It is often said that the character is ambiguous, and different critics emphasise different aspects of her personality and consequently arrive at different evaluations of her. In the end one's judgement of her depends, of course, on one's own values.

The student of *Mrs Dalloway* will find it much easier and more satisfying to read the novel if he or she understands that the ambiguity surrounding Mrs Dalloway does not necessarily arise from careless reading. In fact, the greater one's attention to the detail of the novel, the more one finds that it is impossible to pin Mrs Dalloway down or sum her up. When it comes to answering examination questions, the student should be ready to demonstrate detailed knowledge of the text without necessarily feeling prepared to offer a definite view or final judgement on all aspects of Clarissa's character. Because this is such a central aspect of the novel, there are given here, to help in guiding the student's reading, some notes on the main areas of ambiguity in the life and character of Clarissa Dalloway.

Virginia Woolf at one point herself almost gave up writing *Mrs Dalloway* because she found Clarissa Dalloway too lacking in interest, too superficial. She noted in her diary, 'the doubtful point is, I think, the character of Mrs Dalloway. It may be too stiff, too glittering and tinselly'. Sometimes, she thought that she positively disliked her. A very perceptive reviewer of the novel argued that Virginia Woolf could not decide whether to laugh at Clarissa or to identify with her and thus take her very seriously. Perhaps in the end she did both. The indecision reflected Virginia Woolf's attitude to the social life of the elite. She sometimes found it attractive and exciting but at the other times she found it trivial, time-wasting and irritating. This is reflected in the shifting tone of the novel. Sometimes Clarissa seems to be a figure of fun and a vehicle for a satire on the triviality and decadence of the social elite. In these passages she is treated in the same satirical spirit as are Hugh Whitbread and Lady Bruton. Look, for example, at the treatment of Clarissa when she is talking in the flower shop with Miss Pym, or when she is thinking about her relations with her servants, or receiving her guests at her party and saying 'How delightful to see you!' to every one of them. There are other passages, however, which have been read as a celebration of life and of female creativity. It is difficult to judge the tone of the section where Clarissa defends her parties against the imagined attacks of the men (pages 108-9), but it can certainly be argued that they are intended seriously, and not ironically, as an assertion of female values. 'Could any man understand what she meant . . . about life?', Clarissa wonders; could they understand how giving parties could be a ceremony, an offering? Men's values, which are expressed in such things as war, empire and cricket, are so different that she would not expect them to understand.

This same shifting tone and ambiguity of judgement can be found when it comes to estimating Clarissa's personality. Some critics emphasise and agree with Peter Walsh's verdict that Clarissa suffers from a 'death of the soul' and that she makes 'a perfect hostess', which is to say that she is out of touch with life (politics, intelligence, love, sexuality) and only exists as a kind of empty public mask or performance (effusive hypocrisy). Others emphasise the opposite view, and find that Clarissa is predominantly a courageous woman who, unlike the more superficial characters, does not suffer from self-deception and false pride, and is not blind to the facts of human life. She is aware of the pain, agony, loneliness, grief and illness that people suffer and spends her life attempting to alleviate that suffering in her own way.

On this view, the female arts of relationship-building and attentiveness are the basis of civilisation, the flowers in the dungeon (in Clarissa's image, page 70) that make life tolerable. As for love and sexuality, it has been noted (above, in Part 3, section on 'Characters') that a similar difference of emphasis exists here. Is frigidity unhealthy and neurotic or is it a mature preservation of independence? Is it life or death of the soul? It should be noted that on each of these issues, Clarissa herself holds, at different times during the day, each of the different opinions in turn. Phyllis Rose says 'I read *Mrs Dalloway* as celebration, not as satire—a celebration of the ecstasy of living and an elegy for the swift passage of that ecstasy.'* On the other hand, Hermione Lee remarks, that 'Clarissa's "offering", her "triumph", her attempt to "kindle and illuminate", on which the book converges, is seen as hollow, trivial and corrupt, providing satisfaction for the least satisfactory part of her character'.** The vital point, for the student, is not to be disconcerted by these differences.

---

* Phyllis Rose, *Woman of Letters: A Life of Virginia Woolf*, Routledge and Kegan Paul, London, 1978, p.125.
** Hermione Lee, *The Novels of Virginia Woolf*, Methuen, London, 1977, p.106.

Part 5

# Suggestions for further reading

## The text

The edition of Virginia Woolf's *Mrs Dalloway* used in these Notes is the paperback published as a Triad Panther book by Granada Publishing Ltd, London, in 1976 with numerous subsequent reprints. A paperback edition of the text is published in the U.S.A. by Harcourt Brace Jovanovich Inc., New York, 1964. Virginia Woolf's Introduction to *Mrs Dalloway* was published in an American edition, Modern Library Series, New York, 1928.

## Other works by Virginia Woolf

*Mrs Dalloway's Party: A Short Story Sequence*, ed. Stella McNichol, Hogarth Press, London, 1973. A paperback edition is published in the U.S.A. as a Harvest Book by Harcourt Brace Jovanovich, New York, 1975.
*To the Lighthouse*, Triad Panther Books, London, 1977 (paperback): probably Virginia Woolf's most widely read novel.
*A Room of One's Own*, Hogarth Press, London 1928; Triad Panther Books, London, 1977 (paperback). This is Virginia Woolf's witty campaigning book on women and writing, written a few years after *Mrs Dalloway*.
*Moments of Being*, ed. Jeanne Schulkind, Sussex University Press/Chatto and Windus, London, 1976; Triad Panther Books, London 1978 (paperback).
*Virginia Woolf's Diary*, ed. A. O. Bell, Hogarth Press, London; Penguin Books, Harmondsworth. The titles are as follows, the first date in brackets indicating the Hogarth Press edition, the second the Penguin: Vol. I, 1915-1919 (1977; 1979); Vol. II, 1920-4 (1978; 1981); Vol. III, 1925-30 (1980; 1982); Vol. IV, 1931-5 (1982; 1983); Vol. V, 1936-41 (1984). See especially Volumes II, 1920-4, and III, 1925-30.
*A Writer's Diary*, ed. Leonard Woolf, Hogarth Press, London, 1953; paperback edition published by Triad Panther Books, London,

1978. This contains extracts from the *Diaries* pertaining to Virginia Woolf's writings, selected by her husband.

## Biographies

BELL, QUENTIN: *Virginia Woolf, A Biography*, 2 vols., Hogarth Press, London, 1972; paperback edition published by Paladin Books, London, 1976.

GORDON, LYNDALL: *Virginia Woolf: A Writer's Life*, Oxford University Press, Oxford, 1984.

POOLE, ROGER: *The Unknown Virginia Woolf*, Cambridge University Press, Cambridge, 1978; paperback edition published by Harvester Press, Brighton, 1982. This book contains the most thorough treatment of Virginia Woolf's 'madness', though its conclusions are widely disputed by other scholars.

## Criticism

GUIGUET, JEAN: *Virginia Woolf and her Works*, translated by Jean Stewart, Hogarth Press, London, 1965.

HAWTHORN, JEREMY: *Virginia Woolf's Mrs Dalloway: A Study in Alienation*, Sussex University Press/Chatto and Windus, London, 1975 (paperback).

LEE, HERMIONE: *The Novels of Virginia Woolf*, Methuen, London, 1977 (both hardback and paperback editions).

LOVE, JEAN: *Virginia Woolf: Sources of Madness and Art*, University of California Press, Berkeley and London, 1977.

ROSE, PHYLLIS: *Woman of Letters: A Life of Virginia Woolf*, Routledge and Kegan Paul, London, 1978: an excellent feminist treatment of Virginia Woolf's life and works; chapter 7 is on *Mrs Dalloway*.

# The author of these notes

JOHN MEPHAM was educated at Oxford and Princeton Universities. He taught philosophy for many years at the University of Sussex, and has also taught at colleges in the U.S.A. and Australia. He lives in London.